S0-ARH-474

Sara

Sara

Eva Gibson

BETHANY HOUSE PUBLISHERS
MINNEAPOLIS, MINNESOTA 55438
A Division of Bethany Fellowship, Inc.

Scripture quotations are taken from the *New American Standard Bible*

Library of Congress Catalog Card Number 84–71717

ISBN 0–87123–598–6

Copyright © 1984
Eva Gibson
All Rights Reserved

Published by Bethany House Publishers
A Division of Bethany Fellowship, Inc.
6820 Auto Club Road, Minneapolis, Minnesota 55438

Printed in the United States of America

Dedicated to the men in my life:
My husband, Bud,
My sons,
Mark
Darren
Dow
Alan
Guy

Springflower Books (for girls 12–15):

Melissa
Michelle
Lisa
Sara
Erica
Jill

Heartsong Books (for young adults):

Kara
Jenny
Andrea
Anne
Karen
Carrie
Colleen
Sherri

EVA GIBSON, a homemaker with six children, is active in a Baptist church in Sherwood, Oregon. She is a free-lance writer whose articles have been published in several youth periodicals. Her first two books are *Melissa* and *Michelle*.

Table of Contents

1 / Forbidden Date

"You don't have to shake," Sara admonished her trembling hands, applying mascara to her curling lashes.

But her hands refused to obey. A dab of mascara spotted beneath her artfully lined brows.

She picked up a tissue and rubbed gently. Suddenly her door swung open. She jumped, her hand knocking a perfume bottle onto the floor.

Sara's blond eight-year-old sister, Amanda, stood framed against the hall darkness, her big, blue eyes blinking in the lamplight.

"Sara," she said uncertainly.

The tissue dropped from Sara's hand. "Mandy," she scolded. She bent to pick up the bottle. "It's after 10:30! What are you doing roaming around in the night?"

"I—I had a dream. Can I come in? Please?"

Sara started to shake her head, then relented. "All right," she said grudgingly, "for a minute."

But the little girl stood motionless in the doorway. "Why aren't you in your nightgown, Sara?"

"Because—" Sara tossed her head in sudden defiance. "I just wanted to see what I look like dressed—like this. For fun—"

She turned to the mirror again, examining her reflection. Sara stared back at herself.

Yet Sara *wasn't* herself, really. The light sprinkling of freckles over her upturned nose were covered with makeup. The gray depths of her eyes, enhanced with shadow and mascara, shone from her oval-shaped face framed by shoulder-length brown hair.

But it was her open-necked black shirt splashed with red

roses that made her catch her breath. Somehow it accentuated the curve of her breast, the loveliness of her throat.

"I don't like your blouse," Mandy said, flipping her long, blond hair. "It doesn't go with your gold cross."

Sara's hand rose involuntarily, covering the gold pendant she'd worn so long. "Amanda Rose Faulkner, just because you're my little sister doesn't give you the right to say unkind things about—about the way I look!"

Mandy's blue eyes dropped their searching gaze. "I'm sorry," she whispered, "you just seemed so strange—not yourself at all. And I—" The little girl turned and ran from the room.

"Mandy!" Sara cried. "The little terror," she muttered beneath her breath. She grabbed her blue robe, pulling it on over her silk shirt and designer jeans.

Sara found Mandy curled up in bed, her face buried in the pillow, muffling her sobs. Gently she cradled her sister against the old familiar robe.

"Hey, little creep. It's okay, okay—"

But it wasn't.

"Sara, are you going out?" Mandy choked.

Sara bit her lip. "No," she said, but inside, her thoughts clamored. *Liar, liar. You're dating someone your parents would never approve of. And no one knows—except Boyd.*

She bent over the little girl. "Listen, Pet. If you'll stop crying and go right to sleep, I'll give you something. Something special."

Mandy's sobs quieted. She turned her face toward her sister. Something inside Sara softened as she saw Mandy's wet lashes stuck into little teepees.

Gently she smoothed the tangled hair away from Mandy's damp forehead. With sudden decision she unhooked the gold pendant and slid it around her sister's neck. She kissed her quickly. "Not another word," she said.

Sara hurried back to her own room and glanced at the clock. It was after eleven. For a moment she hesitated. Wouldn't it be better to just crawl into bed?

She caught a glimpse of her reflection in the mirror.

Slim, alive, sixteen—too old to be cooped up forever with a family who didn't understand—roped in with smooth platitudes and a love that corralled her like a colt crazy for freedom.

Sara caught her breath. Her throat looked naked without her cross catching the familiar lamplight, shimmering gold. She turned away, jerking open her jewelry box drawer.

When she crept down the stairs a few minutes later, a tiny silver butterfly nestled in the cross's place. Her fingers reached up, touching the filigree outline, feeling the pulse of fear throbbing in her throat.

She paused halfway down the stairs. Her parents' room had been built out over the garage at a later date than the rest of the house, separating it from the main part. There was only silence behind the closed door. Sara pulled her white cardigan sweater closer. *Liar, sneak!* her thoughts cried.

She refused to listen. Muting her footsteps, she continued down the stairs, through the hall, and into the basement. Her fingers groped for the light switch. Lights blazed overhead, bringing into sharp relief the outlines of washer and dryer, the clothes horse pushed against the wall, shelves of home-canned peaches and preserves, a crazy assortment of boxes.

Her steps quickened as she passed them, heading for the door that opened into the tunnel connecting the house to the street. For a moment she fumbled with the key, then pushed the door open and extinguished the light.

The tunnel was dark. Only a subdued light from its opening gave her direction. Her feet stumbled on the rough cement. A breeze from the outside blew toward her, making goose bumps run along her arms.

"Fool," she whispered, "this isn't freedom. It's foolishness!"

Still she kept on. She could see better now since the moon had risen, mingling its soft light with the harsh streetlights. The overhanging ivy growing around the tunnel opening cast shifting shadows along the walls. So beautiful and yet . . .

At the tunnel's end, she reached out an uncertain hand, parting the ivy tendrils. The street climbed the hill away from her, light and dark mingling into a still-life tapestry.

Across the street, windows gushed harsh light into the summer night. High above, an oak tree waved its branches restlessly.

Her heart pounded in apprehension. *Would he come?* The beams of an approaching car cut through the darkness. Sara swallowed hard. *Was it Boyd?*

Disappointment enveloped her as a bulky station wagon passed, slowly lumbering up the hill. The ivy dropped from her hand. She leaned back, shoving her shoulders against the hard, unyielding cement wall.

She could feel its roughness through her sweater and flowered silk blouse. Her hand crept up, fingering the frail butterfly.

"Roses and butterflies," she whispered, "somehow they don't go with dark tunnels."

The sound of a motorcycle throbbed in the darkness. Another car . . .

Sara leaned forward and thrust her head through the tunnel opening. The ivy cascaded around her shoulders, tangling with her brown hair. A green-leaved tendril fell over her forehead across her eyes. Impatiently, she flicked it aside.

Headlights glinted on the handle bars of the cycle, silhouetting a helmeted rider as an on-coming car swayed around the corner.

Tires screeched. Suddenly, car and cyclist collided. As in a dream, Sara saw the rider thrown in an arc over the car's hood and the car careen against the light post.

She screamed. Darkness descended. For an instant her body seemed paralyzed with shock. Horror cemented her feet to the tunnel floor.

The car crashed to a stop. She heard the door open, the sound of running footsteps. Then the door slammed shut, the engine roared, and tires screamed their agony.

The car tore away into the night, leaving an empty street with only a crushed motorcycle reflecting the cold moonlight.

Sara leaped forward through the opening, the clinging ivy pulling at her neck and shoulders. Impatiently, she thrust it aside. She must get to the injured cyclist!

She raced up the hill, her breath coming in little nervous gasps, fear making her mouth dry. *Was the cyclist dead?* Had the one who'd struck him down been Boyd, her forbidden date?

Horror welled up in her throat. *Oh, God,* her thoughts cried. *Oh, God, help!*

The cyclist lay beside the road, face down. Sara knelt beside him. A quiet strength she didn't know she possessed rose inside her.

She slid her hand beneath his head, turning it slightly to one side. Her fingers explored his face, hovering before his mouth and nose. Her heart leaped as she felt the warmth of his breath.

She bent lower. "Are you all right?" she whispered.

The man's eyelids fluttered. He licked his lips.

He's young, Sara thought, noting the smooth cheek, the firm chin, the barely discernible mustache.

She touched his forehead. "You're not alone," she said. "My name is Sara. I'll try to stay with you, but somehow we have to get help."

His eyes were open now, watching her. Alarm leaped into them. "No," he whispered, "don't leave me." His voice lowered even further. Sara thought she heard him add, "alone."

Pain wrenched his face, and he rolled clumsily onto his side. "My hand—"

Sara gasped. Blood pulsated from his wrist, staining his fingers. She jerked her sweater off her shoulders and bound it snugly around the injured hand, elevating it.

Someone come quick. Come quick! her thoughts screamed. She looked down at his pale face. His eyes closed in apparent pain. Should she stay? Run for help?

Lights blossomed in the downstairs window of her house. Her chin jerked. Had her parents heard the crash?

A car turned the corner, flooding her in brightness.

Frantically she waved her hand. "Stop!" she screamed. "Stop!"

This time the screech of tires comforted her. A heavyset man hurried toward her.

"Call an ambulance!" she shouted. "He's hurt." She pointed to her house. "There's a phone there—"

The man ran back to his car. Sara watched him drive to her house and stop.

Once again she bent over the injured young man. His breath was shallow. Her white sweater around his wrist rapidly darkened in the moonlight. "He's gone for help," Sara said. "He'll call an ambulance—get you to a hospital."

The man's eyes opened again. Sara saw a great weariness in their shadowed depths.

"Thanks," he murmured. "You're an angel." Once more his eyelids closed.

Sara's lips trembled. *Oh, no, I'm not!* she wanted to cry. *If you only knew!*

Instead she said, "My house is close. He went there to telephone." *Oh, hurry!* she cried inwardly as she noted the stain widening on her sweater. Aloud she said, "They're coming! Dad's with them!"

"Sara!" her father cried. "Sara?"

"Yes. Come quickly!"

He was beside her in a moment, his hand under hers, relieving her of the weight of the man's arm. "I've called an ambulance," he said.

The young man's eyes opened. "Police?"

Her father nodded. "They'll want to find out what happened. Do you know?"

The heavyset man who had brought her father pushed forward. He was broad-shouldered and dressed in tan coveralls that zipped to the neck. His small eyes, embedded in his beefy face, snapped with excitement.

"Your motorcycle is a total wreck. What hit you?"

The weary eyes opened again, then closed. "I—I didn't see. I can't remember. I—"

Sara touched his cheek lightly. "Don't worry right now," she pleaded. "Later."

The beefy man's hand smashed down hard on her shoulder. "What about you? Did you see anything?"

A strange iciness settled into Sara's stomach. "I—"

His hand tightened and Sara winced.

"Where were you when it happened, anyway?" the man asked.

"Sara?" Her father seemed to echo the question.

Sara pulled her attention away from the injured man and looked at her father—a tall man with thick, dark eyebrows, casually dressed in blue jeans and an unbuttoned flannel shirt. A questioning frown cloaked his face. She sensed his fear as he probed the tense lines in her face. But she could only shake her head.

The whine of a siren cut through the night, growing louder and louder.

"Sara," her father's low voice entreated. His intense hazel eyes riveted on her.

Sara bit her lip. Was he noticing her carefully made-up face, her silk blouse, her snug designer jeans?

She felt an unexpected longing for her cardigan sweater or her brown suede jacket from her room.

A police car and a rescue squad, their red-blue lights flashing, veered simultaneously around the corner. Sara leaned over the injured cyclist and whispered, "They're here. You'll be all right now."

Two men from the emergency vehicle converged around him as she stepped back. An authoritative-looking young policeman took charge as an ambulance rolled to a halt beside the other vehicles.

The policeman's questions and loud explanations from the man in the coveralls blended into confusion. Two attendants appeared with a stretcher and lifted the injured man onto it. Sara had a fleeting last glimpse of his pale face with closed eyes. She buried her head in her father's arm.

She shivered. Tears burned her eyes as her father pulled the soft folds of his flannel shirt around her shoulders.

She looked up. "Dad," she whispered, gesturing toward the crumpled cycle. "It's partly my fault. I—I—"

The policeman pushed close. "Were you a witness to the accident?" he asked Sara.

Sara's eyes never faltered from her father's. "Yes."

"Your name?"

"Sara Faulkner." Even as she answered, she saw hurt flare in her father's eyes. "I'm sorry, Dad," she blurted. "But I was waiting, hiding in our tunnel, looking out when that car came around the corner and—"

The officer's pen flicked impatiently. "What kind of car was it?"

"Light-colored. I'm not sure."

"License number?"

Sara shook her head.

"Did you see a face? Anything you could identify?"

"No—except I think"—her words came out in a rush—"he might be someone named Boyd." Sara's agonized eyes sought her father's. "I was going to go out with him, and—"

The policeman put his pen down. "Never came, huh?"

"I—I don't know. Whoever hit the cyclist—"

"Matt Roberts is his name," the officer interrupted. "Go on."

"The driver of the car stopped for a minute, opened the door, and ran over to—Matt. Then all of a sudden he rushed back and revved his engine—"

"Took off?"

Sara nodded.

"This Boyd," the officer pursued. "What's his last name?"

"I don't know. He never told me. I shouldn't have said I'd meet him, but I did."

"You're not sure if the person who hit Matt was really Boyd?"

"No," Sara whispered. "It could have been, but I just don't know."

Carefully, she gave him Boyd's description: dark eyes,

brown hair, well-built shoulders, his catlike swaggering stride. "He comes over to the drive-in where I work, and we talk sometimes."

"What kind of car?"

"Different ones. Once it was a Pontiac—dark green. Another time he drove a blue convertible. He said he worked at a used car lot."

"Know where?"

Sara shook her head helplessly. "No, I don't."

The officer wrote down his name and telephone number, then handed it to her. "Thank you, Miss Faulkner. If you think of anything else—"

Sara nodded. "I'll call—really I will."

She and her father watched the officer drive away. The curious heavyset man in coveralls had disappeared in the confusion. A pickup hauled away the damaged motorcycle. The street that had throbbed with action moments earlier was now quiet.

Sara pulled her father's shirt closer around her. It's warmth and softness comforted her, reminding her of his love and care. With that awareness came a sharp pain. Tonight her parents would know all the ugly details. She had failed to live up to their trust. And that wasn't all.

She started to reach for the pendant at her neck. Her fingers stopped in midair. The golden smoothness of the cross was no longer there to remind her that she was a child of the King.

She swallowed hard. Her stomach curled into a hard, cold ball. "Dad," she whispered. "Oh, Dad."

2 / Searching for Silver Wings

"I thought I was strong!" Sara cried. "I thought I could just flirt and have fun, but it didn't turn out that way—"

She turned to her white-faced mother, sitting immobile on the couch. "I knew Boyd wasn't the kind of boy I should date. But I was so tired of—of—the proper guys—the safe ones you approved of."

Sara fell silent. How could she put into words the feelings writhing inside her?—her longing to break into a world with a forbidden touch—a hint of danger. Yet she fought with another longing—to become the daughter her parents would be proud of, to live for the Christ she'd invited into her life when she was in junior high.

"I know I've blown it," she said bravely. "I've failed you and myself, but most of all I've failed the Lord." She looked her father squarely in the eye. "I know that if Boyd was the driver of that runaway car, then in a sense I'm responsible for what happened to that boy, Matt."

"Just a minute, Sara." Her father sat down heavily beside his wife, a tiny muscle in his cheek twitching involuntarily. Sara saw him reach for her mother's hand, saw her trembling one tighten and cling.

"We don't know that—not yet," her father continued. "If Boyd is the sort of boy I suspect he is, he might not have intended to show up."

A flush rose into Sara's cheeks. She stared at her parents' clasped hands. Her father's hand—big, broad across the back but short-fingered; her mother's—slender, sensitive. Her long-sleeved ruffled blue nightgown flared around her small, graceful wrists.

Mrs. Faulkner suddenly stood, releasing her husband's

hand. She paced to the piano, nervously leafed through the piled sheet music, then came back to the couch. She ran her fingers along the edge of the coffee table.

As she looked up, her blue eyes reflected her flowing gown. Or were they bluer than usual because of the shadowy umber circles beneath them and the worry crinkles knitting her forehead?

"Hit-and-run is a serious offense, Sara," she said, smoothing a wisp of her short brown hair into place. "I hate having you involved, even as a witness."

"But I am involved! I didn't see anyone I could identify—" Sara cried, "not really. But I was there."

I should have run away or stayed hidden in the ivy tunnel, she thought. *Then no one would have known—ever.*

Her father spoke. "She didn't see anything, Carol. The lights went out. And she did help the injured boy. If she hadn't, who knows?" His heavy dark brows drew together. "I have to admit I was shocked and sick with disappointment when I found her there—dressed like—"

Tiny pinpricks of shame exploded through Sara's body. She leaped to her feet, thrusting her father's shirt onto the nearest chair.

"You don't understand!" she cried. "You don't even want to understand!"

She raced from the room, her father's voice following her. "Wait a minute, Sara—"

But Sara couldn't wait. She pounded up the steps and into her room, tearing off the silk shirt, wadding it into a ball, and thrusting it into the back of the closet—as far out of sight as she could. Her blue jeans landed in a heap at the foot of her bed.

She grabbed a flowered print nightgown and ran down the hall to the bathroom where she scrubbed off every trace of makeup. Moments later, she lay in the darkness of her room, curled in a tight ball in the middle of her bed. Her hands trembled as she clasped her knees close to her chest.

There was a knock on the door. "Sara," her mother called, "may I come in?"

Sara sat up. "Please—" she choked, "couldn't it wait until morning?"

A pause. "All right, dear, but remember, we love you very, very much."

The soft sound of her mother's footsteps padded on the stairs. Sara almost went after her, just to feel her mother's arms around her.

Instead, she retreated into the middle of her bed, the silent house brooding around her. Pictures flashed before her—the glint of the cross at her throat, Amanda in the doorway, her long nightgown trailing . . . Sara reached up to touch the fragile butterfly. It was gone.

She swallowed hard. Funny, the butterfly hadn't seemed important when she'd first put it on. But now it did.

The words her father had spoken as he'd clasped it around her neck on the night of her eighth grade honor evening flooded through her. "I'm so pleased with your progress, Sara. You're a daughter to be proud of."

Her father was a man of few words. But that only made what he did say more important. Her mind replayed his admission earlier that evening: "I was shocked and sick with disappointment when I found her there."

Sara couldn't sleep. Turning over, she reached for the switch on her bedside lamp. A warm glow filled the room, accentuating her golden stuffed Garfield cat crouched on the rainbow-colored pillows in the corner. Her duck collection paraded proudly on the windowsill.

She slid out of bed and prowled around the room, shaking out her jeans, searching among the bottles on her dressing table.

She walked down the hall into the bathroom, her gaze probing the floor. But no silver glint of intricate filigree could be found anywhere on the hall's earthen brown rug nor among the tufts of yellow carpet in her room.

After a while she crept into bed. Tomorrow she would retrace her footsteps to the top of the hill.

Impulsively, she grabbed a note pad from her bedside table and quickly sketched a delicate butterfly. Somehow, sketching relaxed her. At last she could sleep.

That night Sara dreamed. A butterfly with silver wings flew over a green meadow dotted with lavender mountain asters. A snowy mountain brooded behind it.

Then the dream changed. Lights flashed, sirens screamed, and—there was bright red blood on the snow.

Sara sat up, clasping her knees, her heart pounding. There was no mountain, no fluttering butterfly. "But there was blood," she whispered, "on my white sweater."

She got out of bed and moved to the window, pushing back the violet-hued curtains. The lights of Portland glowed before her. She knew that a little to the left, hidden by houses and trees, stood Mount St. Helens. Looming straight ahead, covered by darkness, Mount Hood's snowy slopes rose unseen into the skyline. It was the silent sentinal of the City of Roses, her home since she'd started high school two years ago.

Suddenly, Sara wished she could leave the noisy streets behind. There were meadows at Mount Hood, hidden lakes, alpine trails . . .

But not yet. She needed to make decisions, resolve the torment that had risen within her. Regret mingled with hot waves of rebellion. Together, they poured through her, scalding her emotions.

She thought of Boyd—the way he'd smiled—walked. "How could I have been so gullible?" she whispered. "Do I really want that kind of guy?"

She went back to bed, but not to think of Boyd. A new face wandered through her thoughts. Matt—the smooth thrust of his chin, the boyish mustache, the weary eyes. She wondered if he were all right.

By morning Sara's confusion had quieted, but she wakened feeling as though she hadn't slept at all. Her gray eyes were clear, her thoughts brittle and sharp with self-judgment.

She hated to get up and face the new day—Mandy, her parents, going to work in the late morning, smiling, lifting an eyebrow, writing an order, chatting with the customers.

Slowly she pushed back her rainbow bedspread, pressed her feet into the soft, deep yellow carpet. "Yellow for joy," Mandy had said. *No, yellow to match a summer morning, to contrast with a night flooded with noise and pain*, she thought.

Quickly, Sara selected gray corduroy slacks and a pink-and-gray-plaid blouse. She would call the hospital, find out how badly Matt had been hurt, and whether or not he was still there.

After she'd called, she'd retrace her steps and try to find the missing butterfly.

The lady at the hospital was helpful, immediately transferring her call to the proper nurses' station.

"He's in room 203 and recovering nicely from his surgery," the nurse informed her.

Sara licked her lips. "Surgery?"

"On his hand. Nothing too serious," the nurse assured her. "May I ask who's calling?"

"Just Sara. Can he have visitors?"

The nurse laughed softly. "Not right now. He's sleeping. But this evening he'll welcome you, I'm sure."

Sara thanked the nurse and hung up. She turned. Her mother stood in the doorway watching her. A hesitant, uncertain look veiled her eyes. She started to say something, then stopped.

Regretfully, Sara read the disappointment in her mother's quivering lips. A rush of shame poured over her. "Matt's all right," she said. "Mother, about last night—"

Her mother nodded wordlessly. Her hand trembled as it covered her mouth.

Sara leaped to her side, her hands on her mother's shoulders. "Mom," she pleaded, "I'm sorry. So sorry—"

For a moment she pushed her face into the furry red fabric of her mother's bathrobe and felt her mom's hand gently touch her hair.

"Oh, Sara, Sara," she murmured. "I didn't sleep all night. I kept worrying, wondering—"

Sara's head jerked back. Sudden hardness crept into her

voice. "You mean you won't trust me now?" Her voice caught. "Ever?"

"Sara!" her mother cried. "I didn't say that! Don't put words into my mouth that I haven't even thought of!"

"I—I'm sorry." Sara looked down, carefully adjusting her belt and tucking in her blouse. "Did Dad say I'm grounded?"

Her mother turned toward the cupboard over the oven and pulled out a box of cornflakes. "No . . . he didn't. In fact, he was horribly quiet. He seems hurt, Sara. You need to show him—"

"I know," Sara said quickly. She blinked. The cheerful red-and-white-checked tablecloth mocked her. So did the morning sunlight pouring over the white sugar bowl and creamer, the centerpiece of white Shasta daisies smiling up at her.

Dad's hurt, she thought, envisioning him going to work with bowed shoulders.

Mom's cast iron skillet clattered against the stove.

"Don't fix anything for me, Mom," Sara mumbled. "I'm not hungry." She hurried out of the kitchen, almost colliding with her little sister.

"Sara!" Mandy cried. "Are you going outside? Can I come, too?" Her blond head tilted beseechingly. Her dimples flashed. "Please?"

Sara swallowed. "I was just going to the top of the hill," she said with a wry smile, "on a butterfly hunt. Of course you can come. But ask Mom. She's fixing breakfast."

Mandy disappeared into the kitchen. Sara roamed restlessly around the living room, observing its familiar details: Dad's black vinyl lounge chair with the newspapers still sprawled on the floor beside it, Mother's old-fashioned piano in the corner, Mandy's paper cutouts strewn over the coffee table, her own lavender sweater carelessly tossed over the back of the couch.

Mandy dashed from the kitchen. "She says okay. She'll wait to cook the eggs."

"You mean just to the top of the hill, don't you, Sara?" Mother called.

"Yes! We'll only be gone a little while." She turned to Mandy. "I lost my silver butterfly and chain," she said as they stepped onto the porch.

"Where?" Mandy asked. "Here?"

"I don't know, silly. Maybe on the sidewalk." She gestured up the hill. "Or in the grass up there."

As they walked, Sara recounted the sights and sounds of the accident and how she happened to see it. She described the crumpled motorcycle and the ambulance. She told her little sister about everything except Boyd and the part he may have played in it.

Mandy's reasoning was razor sharp. "You shouldn't have gone out alone last night. You *were* alone, weren't you?"

"Yes," Sara admitted slowly, "right out here."

Mandy looked thoughtful. "I'm glad you gave me your cross." She pushed the collar of her blue blouse aside. The gold cross shone brightly against her tanned skin. She smiled suddenly. "If you don't find your butterfly, I'll give it back to you."

"Keep your eyes open," Sara reminded. "My butterfly could have fallen in the grass or—"

"Into a crack?" Mandy suggested.

They were silent, their eyes examining the sidewalk and the closely-clipped green grass bordering it. At the scene of the accident, Sara's gaze swept over the tire skid marks and the matted grass where Matt had lain. She shivered as she noted the dark stains on the green.

She turned to the high side of the bank. And there, just where the grass gave way to earth, she saw something black, partially jammed into the ground. She picked it up, brushing dirt from its side.

"It's somebody's camera!" she cried. "Do you suppose?"

"Suppose what?" Mandy asked.

"That this might belong to Matt? It isn't far from where his motorcycle landed."

"Matt?"

"The boy who was hurt," Sara explained patiently. "He was thrown one way, his bike another."

"And his camera another?"

"Probably. Come on, let's go back."

"But we haven't found your butterfly," Mandy protested.

"I know. Maybe it'll turn up in the house. I'm not through yet."

Mandy nodded and raced down the hill, her pale hair flickering with leaf patterns from the artful combination of morning sun and shadowing trees.

Slowly Sara unsnapped the case. "A Minolta," she murmured. "I wonder if Matt is a photography nut."

A surge of unexpected happiness swept through her. She could take the camera to him. She would see him again.

She returned the camera to its case, swung the strap over her shoulder, and hurried down the hill. Instead of joining her mother and sister in the house, she pushed aside the overhanging ivy from the shadowy tunnel entrance, ducked her head, and stepped inside.

There were no delicate butterfly wings to welcome her, only cold gray cement and gritty dust. How different it was in the bold morning light—ugly, uninviting. She shivered as she saw herself stripped of pretense, cheap, huddling in a tunnel, waiting for a boy she hardly knew.

The ivy stirred into a whisper as she stole down the tunnel, then back again. Remembering the previous night's moonlight, she pushed the leaves aside and looked up the hill.

She gasped and shrank back. A boy in his twenties—tall, lean, and very blond—bent over the tire marks. She watched as he stepped onto the grass. He appeared to be searching for something along the bank and surrounding area.

Sara touched the camera case while her thoughts scuttled

frantically. Was the boy merely a curious passer-by? Could he be the hit-and-run driver? Or was he a friend of Boyd's looking for evidence of Boyd's presence last night?

Quickly she memorized the set of his shoulders, the curling fair hair. A shiver ran up her arms as she saw him suddenly stand up straight. His long hawk-like face looked grim as he surveyed her house with a long, meditative stare. Then he turned, strode up the hill and disappeared.

Sara pushed through the ivy and raced after him. If he had a car parked around the corner, unseen . . .

An engine started. Tires screamed. She barely discerned a flash of gray through the leaves.

She stopped, her breath coming in short, ragged gasps. Disappointment hurtled through her. No license number, no evidence of who might have knocked Matt down, and no butterfly either.

She looked down at the camera flopping at her side. At least she had that. She'd take it to Matt when she got off work this evening. Maybe they would have a chance to get better acquainted.

3 / Encroaching Waves

It came from somewhere within herself and hit her almost as hard as a physical blow. *You shouldn't be working here.*

Sara hesitated in the open door of the drive-in, balancing a coffee cup on a serving tray. *That's silly*, she thought. She advanced to the green Chevrolet occupying the #10 slot and fastened the tray onto the open window.

A pair of intense, dark eyes locked her gaze. "I've got more to order, Loveboat," he said in a low, melodious voice that suited his dark hair and sideburns.

He picked up the sugar packet and ripped it open. "I like my coffee the way I like my women—hot and sweet."

A bright pink stole into Sara's cheeks. She lifted her chin and removed her order pad from the deep pocket of her blue apron. "I'll take your order now."

Her cheeks burned as she handed her order to the chef. Lonnie, a quick-moving young man with blue eyes, sandy hair, and too much beard, grinned at her. "Well, Sara, I'm back at the salt mines."

Sara smiled. "How was your vacation?"

Lonnie's beard bobbed as his big hands efficiently steered his spatula over the long grill. "We went to the beach, down toward the California border. Now that's the life!" His spatula waved in the air. "Sand, seagulls, parties, and pretty girls."

Sara turned away. A clamor rose inside her. The rush, the confusion, the casual air of flirtation were pulling her into deepening waters—waters that frightened her.

Quite suddenly, a half-forgotten memory stirred. Mandy, barely four then, had been running on the beach. Closer and

29

closer to the waves she had run. Then as a lacy wave broke on the sand at her feet, she squealed and raced toward her family.

"That wave's running after me. That wave's chasing me!"

Sara's father scopped little Mandy into his arms. "The ocean is like the world," he told her. "It's out to lure us until we're in over our heads. And then, if we keep going out farther and farther, under we go."

Even as young as Sara was, she remembered her mother's quick protest. "Why, Robert, one has to live in it!"

Sara wished she could recall her father's reply.

Doreen tapped her arm. "Hey, Sara, we have customers to please." Sara lifted her head and followed the other girl outside.

The lunch hour gathered in momentum—frosty glasses to fill with Cokes and 7-Up, sandwiches to serve. She forgot her discomfort with "Hot and Sweet" as she kept alert for a blue convertible or a dark-green Pontiac, with Boyd's dark eyes peering through the windshield.

At the end of her shift, she ran to the back room, removed her apron, and combed her hair. She straightened the collar of her pale-blue blouse and touched her throat momentarily, remembering her gold cross, her silver butterfly. Then a quick peek into her purse to be sure the camera was still there, and she was out the door, hurrying to the bus stop.

The bus loomed tall in the street. Just as she stepped aboard she heard a horn honk. She looked across the bus driver's shoulders and caught a glimpse of of a dark-haired man smiling up at her. She was sure it was Hot and Sweet, the leering man from the drive-in. She drew a quick, grateful breath.

Dropping her change into the container, Sara moved to the middle of the bus. She found an empty seat and sank into it, thankful to be away from those suggestive glances.

Once again she opened her purse and looked at the camera. A surge of unexpected pleasure rose in her. *Matt*, she thought, *there's something about him* . . .

Caught away in her private thoughts, time flew. It seemed like only a few minutes later that she stepped off the bus and walked toward the long, white hospital building.

A soft breeze blew in from the river, whipping her brown hair around her face. She tried to smooth it into place as she asked the receptionist for directions to room 203.

The woman gave crisp, clear instructions. "Down the hall, turn left, take the elevator to the second floor. You'll see signs." The receptionist turned to help another woman.

Sara almost tiptoed down the quiet hall, reviewing the "turn left, take the elevator . . ." instructions.

She hesitated in Matt's doorway. Would he recognize her, think it silly she'd come?

He lay looking out the window, his brown hair darker than she remembered. Or was it because of the stark whiteness of the pillow beneath his head?

She cleared her throat nervously and stepped into the room.

Matt turned toward her, a sudden welcoming smile lighting his face. "My angel," he said impishly.

A smile twisted at Sara's lips. "My hero in distress!" she exclaimed. She looked around the room. "How do you like it here?"

Matt's smile folded into a grimace. "Boring." He nodded out the window. "If it weren't for the green trees outside and that pair of arguing crows, I'd have gone stark, raving mad in one day. Actually," he admitted with a rueful smile, "it hasn't been all bad."

"Visitors?"

Matt nodded. "My folks were here. I get to go home in the morning." He tapped his head with his finger. "The doctor wanted to observe me for a while. He said I might have a mild concussion. I told him I was wearing a helmet—"

"You were thrown pretty hard," Sara explained. "If you hadn't had it on, your brains might have been scrambled for good. What about your hand?"

"Nothing much. Just a lot of blood and a lot of sewing." His voice lowered. "I made a mess of your white sweater. Mom took it home to wash."

"That's all right." She hesitated a moment. "Do you suppose she could see if there's a butterfly on a chain caught inside? I lost it last night and I've looked everywhere."

"Special, huh?"

Sara nodded. "Dad gave it to me a long time ago. I guess I didn't realize how much it meant until it was gone."

Matt swung himself into a sitting position, dangling his feet over the edge of the bed. "I'll have her look. Sara— you did say your name was Sara, didn't you?"

"Yes. You remembered!" she replied. "I spell it without an "h"."

"Sara." He rolled it on his tongue, somehow making it sound like music. "Sara. It's like you."

"Like me?"

He grinned. "Someday, maybe I'll explain that." His smile faded. "What I really want to know right now is, what happened there on the hill? The police were here. They told me you were the only one who'd seen anything at all."

Sara leaned forward. "I couldn't tell them much," she admitted. "After the driver hit you, he slammed into a streetlight and everything went black."

"That's what they said."

A sudden flush rose into Sara's cheeks. Matt didn't continue his questioning.

"I think I might know the guy who hit you," she volunteered.

A light flashed in Matt's eyes. "Really?" he exclaimed. "How?"

Sara looked down, her gaze intent on the legs of the bed. "I was waiting for someone," she explained, struggling for words. "It was somebody I wasn't supposed to be seeing. I think it might have been him, but I don't *know* for sure. I didn't really *know* the person I was waiting for, either." She lifted her head.

Matt's eyebrows arched with a question.

"His name is Boyd. I was going to sneak out with him."

Matt's hand reached out and touched hers. "You don't have to tell me, Sara," he said gently.

But I want you to understand! her thoughts cried. "It might be important," she said aloud.

"I agree." He withdrew his hand and banged his heels against the edge of the bed. The rails rattled indignantly. "If I could just get out of this jail—"

"It isn't that bad!"

He laughed. "True. Just the same, I want to get my motorcycle back in working order. And I have a job that's supposed to help send me to college in the fall. If I don't show, they'll probably call someone else."

He turned restlessly. "I'd like to know who hit me. People like that shouldn't be running around. They need to develop responsibility, face up to their actions before they kill someone. That Boyd—"

Sara flinched.

"I'm sorry," Matt apologized. "I shouldn't have mentioned him again."

Sara bit her lip. "It's all right." She studied Matt's face for a moment. *He's different than most of the boys I know, talking about responsibility, facing up to a person's actions.*

"Matt, I almost forgot." She opened her purse, took out the camera, and placed it in his hands.

An admiring whistle escaped him as he unsnapped the case and lifted the camera out. "It's a beauty! But why—?"

"I found it early this morning. It was only a few feet from where your cycle landed, shoved into the bank. I thought it might be yours."

Matt shook his head. "No, it isn't mine. I wish—" He looked up. "I have a similar one at home. A 35mm Canon."

Sara clasped her hands on top of her purse. "I was so sure it would be yours. That's why I came."

"Do you think it might belong to—that Boyd?"

"Maybe. Or someone could have lost it there before the accident."

"Not likely." Matt examined the camera intently. He turned the camera over, rewound the film, then opened the back. "It has black and white film in it. I wonder . . ." He laid it on the sheet and looked up. "I have a darkroom. I'd like to develop this film."

Excitement flooded Sara. "Why, Matt, we might be able to discover the owner of the camera from the pictures!"

"Exactly. If we could get a clue to the identity of that driver—"

Doubt nibbled at Sara. "Shouldn't we turn it in to the police?"

"No, I don't think so. They may not think it's important. After all, it *could* have been lost there earlier. And I'd sure like a stab at solving this myself."

He picked up the case and examined the inside, turning it every direction. "No identification. If it's okay with you, Sara, I'd like to take this film home."

Sara nodded as he removed the film, then handed the camera and case back to her.

"Shall I advertise in the lost and found?" she asked.

He shook his head. "Not yet. We'll see if these pictures show anything." He opened the drawer of his bedside stand and thrust the film inside. "Just keep the camera until I call. I *can* phone you, can't I?"

Sara nodded as she pulled a small note pad and pencil from her purse. She wrote her name and phone number and handed it to him.

"Thanks. How about your address?" He grinned. "I need to return your sweater."

"It's only two houses down from where you crashed, on the same side of the street." She reached for the paper. "But just so you'll know for sure . . ." She added her house number and street, then stood up. "I need to go. I have a bus to catch."

"I appreciate your coming," he said. "A lot. And, Sara, I don't think you're terrible because of Boyd. I want you to know, I think you're special—"

Sara blinked. "Why, Matt, I—"

"Do you go to church, Sara? There's something about you that makes me feel you know the same Lord I do."

Sara swallowed hard. "If you mean the Lord Jesus Christ, I do, Matt. At least I want to know Him better. But these last few months . . ." She sat down again.

"Tell me, Sara."

The words spilled out then—the unrest and confusion, her weariness with the dull routine of church and youth group, coupled with her longings for excitement and adventure. She told him about her job at the Burgermill and her feelings of being drawn into a world that had a strange appeal, yet was oddly lacking.

"Then today I felt I shouldn't be working there." She related her childhood memory of the pounding ocean waves chasing her little sister on the beach.

Matt scowled. "Maybe you're not quite ready for your job, Sara. After all, people swim in the ocean, scuba dive, too. But they don't just plunge in without preparation."

"That's it," Sara sighed. "I don't know how to get ready. At church we've sort of fallen into a rut."

"It's hard when everybody's running a different direction with jobs and school activities."

"It isn't that so much. We've just gotten dull. Me especially."

Matt rubbed his hand against the edge of his water glass. "You need to get back to God, Sara. Really get to know who He is."

"But I don't even have a spark."

"Yes, you do. You asked Him into your life, didn't you?"

Sara nodded

"I know what you mean, though. I had the same problem. Then our youth pastor mentioned that the only way we can get to know Him, really know Him, is by obeying."

"But I try to obey!" Sara cried. "I really do. I even make plans how I'm going to do something His way, and then"—she waved her hands in the air—"I flub it. Instead of kind, gentle words, I say mean, nasty, cutting ones. Or

I run off when Dad's lecturing me.''

"I think it has something to do with our old flesh, Sara,'' Matt explained. "Even though we're Christians, we've still got to deal with it.''

Sara's forehead knitted into a deep frown. She crinkled her nose. "But, Matt, isn't God stronger than me? I know He's inside.''

"Of course He's stronger. But Sara, a lot depends on us. Every day we're choosing activities, making decisions. My mom told me once that our actions depend a lot on the choices we make. Are we going to feed our own desires and wants, or are we going to obey God's voice?''

"What do you mean, 'feed'?''

Matt took a deep breath. "Well, like—'' He groped for words. "If I'm mostly reading garbage, like trashy novels, or even good history books for school, I'm feeding my fleshly nature. But if I'm being careful to read God's Word and let it really search me, then I'm feeding my new nature.''

The frown faded from Sara's forehead. "I can understand that. I really can.''

Matt rubbed his eyebrow thoughtfully. He put his hand down and took another deep breath. His blue-gray gaze wandered out the window.

He needs the outdoors, Sara thought. *Green growing things—birds—*

"It's hard to explain, Sara. Except that more and more, God is becoming a part of my everyday life.'' He smiled. "Now don't go thinking that all I do is sing hymns and read my Bible. I do other things, too.''

"Like riding motorcycles?''

"And camping, backpacking, too.'' He sighed. "And work.''

"Where?'' Sara asked.

"I have a student position in the housekeeping department of a mental hospital. Walls, furniture, quiet rooms— they all get my faithful scrubbing.''

"What's a quiet room?''

"A room where they put really disturbed patients. It

keeps them separate from the rest of the ward so they can't hurt themselves or anybody else.''

''And I'm complaining about my job!'' Sara exclaimed. ''Yours must be something else!'' She stood up, walked to the window and stared outside.

''What are you thinking about, Sara?''

A warmth colored her cheeks. ''This afternoon when I was ordering supplies, I got to thinking about how Joseph ran from Potiphar's wife when she tempted him to sin. And doesn't the book of James say we're to flee temptation?'' She turned to face Matt.

''And yet Paul talked a lot about standing firm and fighting,'' Matt replied. ''I guess what's right one time might be wrong another. I just don't know.''

''Me either.''

''You could be right, though, Sara. Sometimes we have to flee so we have time to grow strong and get to know the Lord better. Have you thought about asking to be transferred to the kitchen?''

''Frying French fries? Lonnie does that.'' She looked out the window again and changed the subject. ''Do you live anywhere near where you crashed?''

''No. We're country folk, tucked in among the trees.''

Sara's eyebrows arched playfully. ''And what were you doing so far from home last night?'' she asked.

''My brother lives in Portland,'' Matt said. He didn't offer any further explanation, and Sara couldn't think of anything to say. The silence grew between them.

''I really must go,'' Sara murmured. Picking up her purse, she impulsively held out her hand. ''Thanks,'' she said with a smile.

Matt squeezed her hand reassuringly. ''I'll call you soon,'' he said.

Somehow, Sara knew he'd keep his word.

The sun still shone through the trees behind Sara's house when she got off the bus. It glimmered on the ivy, touching a gleaming leaf here and there, resting for a moment on a solitary rose poking through the ivy tendrils.

Sara passed the tunnel opening and went up the front steps. Inside, the house was silent.

She climbed the stairs and tossed her purse onto the bed. The open window beckoned, and she stuck her head out.

Her father was working alone in the side yard, hoeing around the roses. He stopped for a moment, his hands clasping the handle, his shoulders bowed.

Regret stabbed Sara. "I've really let him down," she whispered.

She turned and ran down the stairs and out the kitchen door. When her father saw her, a slight smile lighted his serious face.

Sara ran to him and flung her arms around him. Words seemed unnecessary. His strong arms around her shoulders was the only answer she needed. He'd help her know what to do about the waves threatening her.

Later she would ask his advice about trying a different job. Matt would help, too. For the first time in months, she sensed fresh direction and purpose.

Was this the beginning of a new trust based on forgiveness?

4 / Footsteps in the Tunnel

Sara lay in bed absorbing the sounds around her. Cars droned on the distant freeway. An airplane motor throbbed overhead.

Vaguely, Sara wondered what had wakened her. A faint uneasiness stirred within. Her body tensed—listening—waiting—aware of each breath she took.

She heard a faint movement outside. It could be a shrub rubbing against the house, except no breeze ruffled the curtains at the window. Straining to see in the darkness, she observed the faint outline of her dresser. A light reflected in the mirror.

She took a deep breath, and it was almost as if the entire room breathed with her. She sneezed and the illusion shattered. Tossing back the covers, she jumped up and went to the window.

The side yard was bathed in a delicious combination of moon and street light. The top of her dad's tool shed glinted silver, and leaves made mysterious patterns on the grass.

A dark shadow directly beneath her moved stealthily, and a rubbing sound drifted upward. Was someone trying to pry open the kitchen window?

Fear clawed at Sara's throat. She stifled a sudden impulse to toss Garfield on top of the shadow creature and utter a horrid cat squall.

Instead she ran out of her room and down the stairs. "Dad!" she cried, bursting into her parents' room. "Someone's trying to get in the kitchen window!"

The light flashed on. Her father bolted out of bed in one swift motion.

"Sara!" her mother cried, "run upstairs. See if Mandy's okay."

Sara took the steps two at a time. Mandy's room was dark and quiet, the only sound her gentle breathing. Sara backed out and scurried downstairs, almost colliding with her father, who was still in his pajamas.

"No one's there, Sara," he said.

"But I saw something!"

"The light may have frightened them off. We can be thankful." Dad moved into the kitchen, and Sara followed.

"I wish I'd done it," she mumbled.

"Done what?"

"Thrown my Garfield down on his head. I thought about doing it—then making a horrid cat squall."

"Well, I'm glad you didn't," her mother said as she joined them. She sank into a chair at the table, her knee-length crimson duster and long white nightgown floating around her like a variegated camellia blossom. Sara looked down at her own crumpled gown and grimaced.

"Are you going to call the police?" Mother asked.

"Probably," her father replied. "But first I need to make sure there really was somebody out there."

"But—" Sara protested.

"I know, I know. All the same I need to check it out." Dad yanked open a drawer. "Why is it that the flashlight's never here when I need it? Oh, here it is."

Sara pulled an old work coat from the hall closet. "I'm going with you, Dad," she said as she slid the coat's bulkiness around her.

Her father merely grunted as she followed him outside and around the corner of the house. He shot a beam of light onto the kitchen window.

"Paint on the ledge looks kind of scuffed," he said, "but it's hard to tell."

Sara shoved protruding yew branches aside and looked over his shoulder. Her father flashed the light beam onto his watch face, turning it to gleaming gold.

"It seems that 11:30 is prime time for excitement these

days," he said dryly. "Sara, are you sure your—your boy-friend might not have gotten his nights mixed?"

Sara gulped and took a startled step backward. "My boyfriend!" she spluttered. "Do you still think I care about him? After he—he—"

Her father ignored her words as he sent the searching light along the window edges.

"You haven't forgiven me after all, have you?"

Her father half turned toward her. The flashlight beam dropped to the ground below the window. A perfect outline of a foot imprinted the damp earth beneath the water faucet.

Her father bent down, examining it carefully.

Sara crouched beside him, her anger forgotten. "It's too big to be yours," she observed.

"Yes," he agreed. "It's fresh, too." He straightened, slowly playing the light along the edge of the shrubbery. Nothing.

"I'll call the police," he said.

They went back into the house, and her father poked his head into the kitchen. "How about fixing me a cup of your hot, spiced grape juice?"

"There isn't any in the kitchen cupboard," Mother said. Her fingers toyed with the edges of the red placemats. "I'd hate to go down to the basement right now. Did you see anything out there?"

"Just a footprint," her father explained.

"I'll go down and get the juice," Sara volunteered.

"Sara," her mother protested.

But the need for action pulled at her. She lifted the hem of her nightgown and hurried downstairs, ignoring her mother's fear.

Instead of intruders and distrusting fathers, I'll think about the grapes, she decided.

Everyone told them their grapes were in too shady a spot to produce, but the grapes obviously didn't know that. Every year the vines outdid themselves, and every year Mother filled the kitchen with their warm, tangy aroma.

Something magical happened to them when they were

heated inside the juicer. The green juice you'd expect from green grapes transformed into a pale pink. It brought out the beauty of the dark red blackberry jelly and Bing cherries sitting next to it on the shelves.

Sara groped for the light switch. She gasped. The door into the tunnel swung wide, a silent invitation to any intruder.

For a moment Sara's feet refused to move. Then she rushed to the open door. Running footsteps not her own echoed back at her. She peered into the passageway. The ivy at the far end moved, fluttering in a silent plea.

Cautiously, she moved down the tunnel length, muffling her footsteps. At the entrance she stopped and parted the swinging ivy.

The street slept quietly in the subdued light. No breeze whispered in the leaves. No car lumbered up the hill. Whoever had been skulking around their house had disappeared.

She dropped the ivy from her hand and returned. A bar of welcoming light lay across the open doorway, framing a section of the tunnel floor. Something silver glinted in the pool of golden light.

Sara bent down. "My butterfly!" she exclaimed. "It was here all the time."

But was it? She'd searched every inch of the tunnel in broad daylight. She couldn't have missed it!

"But if it wasn't there then, how did it get here now?" she asked no one in particular.

Had Mandy found it and then accidentally dropped it while she was playing? Sara looped the necklace around her finger, shut the door and went over to the fruit shelves. She picked up a jar of pink grape juice and carried it upstairs.

Her father frowned at her. "I was about to go after you," he said. "What took you so long?"

Sara set the jar on the table. "The door to the tunnel was wide open," she said. "I went clear to the end to see if anyone was outside."

"Sara!" her mother gasped, "you shouldn't—"

"No one was there." She said nothing about the butterfly and chain looped around her fingers, nor about the
echoing footsteps.

The scowl on her father's face deepened. "Did you leave
it unlocked last night?" he asked.

"I—I don't think so. Wait, maybe I did." Her own
forehead creased into a troubled furrow.

"We're going to have to be careful to lock all the doors
from now on," her father said. Worry made his voice harsh.
"I don't like the idea of intruders lurking around the house."

"Who does?" Mother asked tartly.

Sara picked up the jar of juice and carried it to the kitchen
counter. "None of us," she muttered. She opened the jar
and poured three cups, added a bit of water to each one,
some cloves, and a teaspoon of brown sugar.

She set them inside the microwave and picked up the
butterfly necklace she'd laid beside the jar. As she hooked
it around her neck she wondered whose hands had last touched
it—Mandy's or— Her own hands froze over the tiny clasp.
Could it have been the hit-and-run driver?

It had been hard to leave the warmth of the kitchen. The
comfortable food smells had closed around Sara and made
her feel safe and somehow confident.

Alone in her room, self-accusation spit icy little pellets
of doubt into her heart. What kind of man was Boyd, anyway? Someone racing from the law? A burglar creeping into
homes? What was her decision to go with him that night
going to cost her, and her parents, and Matt?

"Boyd, Boyd," she whispered, "who are you beneath
that melting grin—those penetrating eyes?"

She caught Garfield's round-eyed, questioning gaze and
grimaced. "I almost tossed you out the window onto his
head," she confided. "Sorry, old friend."

She got into bed and pulled the blanket over her shoulders, trying to quiet her whirling thoughts. It was no use.
She turned over onto her back and stared at the ceiling.

Matt would probably be asleep by now. She smiled as
she remembered his explanation of a Christian feeding either

his fleshly nature or his new, spiritual nature. Her thoughts drew funny pictures of a great, fat "old man" standing over a frail "new man" lying prone at his feet. A huge spoon started to lower toward the skinny man, but just as it reached his lips the fat man's hand came down with a bang. The food spattered in a dozen directions.

Sara sat up. She knew she needed to talk to her parents about her job, try to explain how she felt she was feeding her old nature.

In the meantime, she'd think about God—who He is, what He wanted to do in her life. She slipped out of bed and knelt down beside Garfield on the soft pillows.

"Dear Lord," she whispered, "forgive me for the way I've been starving my spiritual life. Help me to know who you are, who I am. Please, Lord, please."

After a while she climbed back into bed. Her thoughts no longer tormented her. A peace that had nothing to do with her circumstances reached out and cradled her close. Just before sleep claimed her, she wondered if this was the peace that passed human understanding, the kind the Bible talked about.

Sara wakened to a morning sun sliding long golden fingers across the room, seeking excitement in its own glaring reflection in the dressing table mirror. She sat up, surprised and pleased that she had slept so soundly after the previous night's fear. She smiled, remembering the prayer she had prayed beside her yellow cat.

This morning, he almost seemed to be dozing. A rumpled pillow hid his face as the sunshine nested in his yellow fake fur.

Sara tossed back her covers and went to the closet. *Something pastel and lovely to match the day*, she decided, tossing light blue slacks and a sky blue blouse onto the bed.

She stopped. She had told God that she wanted to know Him.

Matt had said that the best way to know God was through reading His Word. She turned to her bookcase. Her Bible, which she'd received years before as a prize for learning the books of the Bible in Sunday school, peeked out between *Menfreya in the Morning* and *The Art of Still Life Painting*.

She pulled it out and sat down in Garfield's pillow nest, opening the Bible on her lap. "Where should I start reading?" she asked the silent stuffed cat.

Mandy rescued her from indecision. Prancing into the room, she stepped in front of the sun's reflection, making faces at herself in the mirror.

Then she dropped into a heap beside Sara, exclaiming, "You've found your butterfly! Where was it?"

Sara cocked her head to one side. "You don't know?"

Mandy's blue eyes stared at her. "No," she said. "Why should I?"

"Oh, I just wondered. It was in the tunnel where I'd looked before."

Mandy was distracted by the open Bible. "Oh!" she exclaimed, "are you reading it?"

Sara tossed her head. "I was—until you popped in—without even knocking."

"I'm sorry." She laid her head on her sister's shoulder, touching the delicate wings that nestled in the hollow of Sara's throat. "I'm reading mine too," she confided, "every morning. I started at the first chapter of John and I'm already at the 'let not your heart be troubled' chapter."

"Which one's that?" Sara asked.

"Fourteen." Mandy jumped up. "I shouldn't have interrupted you. I'm sorry." She dashed across the room. The door closed behind a swirl of ruffled yellow nightgown.

Sara smiled after her. " 'Let not your heart be troubled' might not be a bad place for me to begin," she murmured.

The words she read were Jesus' own. "Let not your heart be troubled; believe in God, believe also in Me.

"In My Father's house are many dwelling places; if it were not so, I would have told you; for I go to prepare a place for you.

"And if I go and prepare a place for you, I will come again, and receive you to Myself; that where I am, there you may be also."

She stopped. They were beautiful words, haunting words. They were telling her what God felt about her! He didn't want her to be afraid. And He loved her so much, He wanted to be with her forever!

She brushed sudden tears from her lashes. How tender God was to send Mandy prancing in with her "let not your heart be troubled" chapter.

Once again Sara bowed her head. Since He loved her, since He cared, she would give her fears and indecision to Him.

5 / Burglary

"Summer jobs aren't that easy to find," Sara's father protested. He leaned forward, nervously drumming his fingers against the arm of the black vinyl chair. "Where would you begin looking?"

"I don't know," Sara said in a small voice. "Maybe at the downtown stores. I could sell dresses, or candy in one of the department stores."

"What makes you think the problems you're having now wouldn't be repeated somewhere else?"

Sara lowered her gaze. Was he right? Were the thoughts she'd discussed with Matt based only on emotion? No, something deep inside told her she was doing the right thing.

"On the other hand, a new start can make a difference," her dad reasoned.

Sara's chin jerked up. "Oh, Dad, I was hoping you'd understand."

Mother sat by the window, filing her nails. She entered the conversation for the first time. "I have an idea. It's probably not what you have in mind, Sara, but I'd like you to consider it."

She toyed with the file, her fingers sliding back and forth along its rough edge. "Since you think the drive-in is wrong for you, and since jobs are hard to get, I'd like you to consider staying home with Mandy this summer."

Her husband raised a hand in quick protest.

"Wait," she entreated. "For months Lucille has been asking me to help in her shop this summer. I've always said no because I needed to be here with Mandy." She lowered her voice, "I wish you'd consider it, Robert. It's something I'd love to do."

47

A vision of Lucille's bridal shop rose into Sara's mind—pastel bridesmaid dresses, ruffled garters with blue ribbons, the big sample books of wedding invitations and napkins. A certain scent pervaded it, too—rose petals and crisp new laces. She could see her mother answering the telephone, taking orders, talking to customers.

"Spring and summer are her busiest times," Mother pursued, "and right now her husband wants to take off for the mountains. She feels torn between him and her business."

Her father's dark brows drew together. "Is it something Sara might do?"

Her mother laid the file down and stood up. "You don't understand, Robert. It's something *I* want to do. And if Sara isn't happy in her job—"

"I see. So that's how the wind blows." He got up and hugged his wife. "Tired of staying home, honey?"

Sara slipped out of the room unnoticed. Her mother's words followed her. "It isn't that. It's just something I'd enjoy. Oh, I don't know. We're such—such plodders. And sometimes I long for pretty things."

Upstairs in her room, Sara tore a piece of paper from her notebook and began to write. "I'm resigning my position." Her halting fingers drew a picture of a tall French fry. She added stick legs and arms and drew in a sad face, then continued, "My last day will be one week from today."

She slipped the paper underneath the edge of her jewelry box and picked up her hairbrush. Her bus would come soon—too soon.

That afternoon at the Burgermill, Sara and Doreen sat together at a small table in the kitchen, an icy orange drink in front of each of them.

"I think you're nuts!" Doreen exclaimed. "I know this isn't the best job in the world, but it's not the worst either." She arched darkened brows at the younger girl. "I can't imagine you having much fun stuck at home baby-sitting your sister. Ugh! Sounds boring."

Sara sighed. "I know. It's not what I planned," her

voice lowered, "but somehow I think it's what God wants."

Doreen tossed her dark hair over her shoulder. "Why, Sara! I didn't know you were religious."

A blaze of pink crawled into Sara's cheeks. "I'm not exactly," she confessed. "But lately my life has been so empty." She gestured toward the drive-in's canopied service lot. "At first it was glamorous, the boys flirting with me, feeling pretty for the first time in my life. But now—"

She stopped. She didn't want to tell the other girl about the accident by her house or the doubts it had raised inside her.

Doreen shrugged. "Well, it's your funeral." A horn honked outside. "My car!" She scrambled outside to serve her customer.

After Doreen left, Sara sat still. Resigning from her job had been easier than she'd thought.

Before she had left for work her father had taken her aside. "Sara," he said, "I'd like you to resign from your job as soon as possible so you can be home to watch Mandy."

Some idiotic perversity within her made her want to say, "So? What if I've changed my mind?" She didn't.

Her father looked at her intently. For the first time Sara noticed the dark circles beneath his eyes, the nervous movement of his hand on the garden trowel he was holding.

"I didn't realize at first how much your mother needed a change. I want to give her a chance to try her skills."

"I'll put in my resignation today," Sara said.

He nodded. "Thanks, Pet."

Now Sara jabbed the bottom of the glass with her straw and sighed deeply. A rough hand clasped her shoulder.

She looked up. Lonnie stood smiling down at her.

"Don't look so unhappy, Kitten. Someday it'll be back to the salt mines. In the meantime"—he raised his hands over his head—"your freedom is there to enjoy!"

"Freedom?" Sara spluttered. "I'll have my little sister under foot every minute."

"So what? You women don't know when you have a good thing." He grinned broadly and lowered his arms.

"You know what my sister says about women leaving their homes for the job market? She says it's part of a male chauvinistic plot.

"So you, dear one, just enjoy those hours when you can be free to—oh, talk on the phone, take a nap, bake a pie—" He went back to his French fries and sizzling burgers, whistling good-naturedly.

Sara smiled. In spite of his sly winks and borderline jokes, Lonnie was a good friend. She'd miss him.

The dinner hour began. Sara put her glass in the dish tray, pinned on her prettiest smile, and looked out the window, involuntarily searching for Boyd, wondering.

He wasn't there, but Matt was. He honked his horn lightly and waved his hand, grinning broadly. She went to him at once, her footsteps quick and eager.

"I was hoping I'd find you here," he said, his steady gray-blue gaze intent. He gestured toward Doreen. "Your friend said you were having a break."

"Which is now officially over. How have you been? How's your hand?"

He raised his arm tentatively. "Good as new—almost. Back to the doctor in a week and off with the bandage. How about a hamburger and Coke?"

"Burger and Coke coming up."

She started to turn away, but Matt stopped her. "Boyd been in?"

Sara shook her head. "What about that roll of film? Have you developed it yet?"

"No. In fact, that's one of the reasons I'm here."

Sara's brows arched curiously. She stood poised, ready to hurry about her tasks, a trim, efficient figure in dark blue slacks and apron, and blue gingham blouse.

"I'd like you to be there when I develop it. I've replenished the fixer and everything's set. When could I pick you up? Or do you want to?"

"Oh, I'd love to see how you develop pictures. Would day after tomorrow be all right? I have a day off." She started to tell him that after the end of the week she'd have lots of time, but she shut her lips determinedly. Later.

Quickly they made arrangements for him to come to the house and meet her parents. "They might not let me because—because of Boyd," she confessed. "But we can at least try."

He nodded in understanding, and Sara hurried inside to give his order to Lonnie. After that, there were more Cokes, hot coffee, hamburgers and a never-ending stream of French fries to serve.

They only had a few brief words before Matt departed. Sara's heart sang. *He makes me feel good about myself,* she thought, *while Boyd, even when I thought he was so special, never did.*

Now when she thought about Boyd, she was reminded of Hot and Sweet. They had the same dark eyes, the same suggestive intentness in their depths. Sara shivered. She thrust her thoughts aside and concentrated instead on clearing trays and serving customers.

It was almost time for her shift to end when she looked out the window and saw a green car that looked familiar. Boyd—but it wasn't Boyd at all. Her lips curled in revulsion as Hot and Sweet smiled at her. Sara was suddenly glad for the glass between them. She stepped back.

Doreen swished through the door. "Your customer, honey."

Sara straightened her shoulders with new purpose. "I'm sorry, Doreen," she said. "I'm off duty in a few minutes. This one's yours."

She turned to the fountain and shot a squirt of chocolate into the milk shake container. The mixer whirled noisily, drowning out Doreen's reply.

Sara laid napkins and a straw on a tray, then reached for the shake. As she carried it outside, she saw Doreen standing at Hot and Sweet's window. She ignored them, her head held high.

As soon as she'd served her last customer, she hurried out of her apron and into her dark blue cardigan. At the back of the room, she stopped and looked outside.

The green Chevrolet still sat there. A wave of unexplained fear swept over her. She sat down abruptly at the table in the kitchen.

"What's the matter, Sara?" Lonnie teased. "Can't you bear to be parted from your job?"

Sara licked her lips nervously. "Not exactly. I'm just hungry, I guess." She smiled mischievously and banged her hand on the table. "How about some service around here? I want a hamburger and lots of French fries. And a milkshake—chocolate."

Lonnie threw up his hands in mock horror, his spatula spattering grease down his apron front. "Coming up, madam. My very best creation. With onion, and pickles, tomatoes, and relish."

"Don't forget the catsup and mustard! And how about a slice of cheese, melted just yummy."

"Girl, why don't you ask for a cheeseburger?" Lonnie slapped a hamburger onto the grill. "But the customer is always right. When you ask for service, you get it. I hope you can pay for this thing."

Sara laughed. "Why, sir, it's on the house. My going away present, if you please."

By the time Lonnie served her, they were both giggling. Sara made a point of lingering over her meal. She didn't slip out the back until she was sure Hot and Sweet was long gone.

She arrived home later than usual. Even before she stepped onto the porch, she heard the musical strains of her mother's favorite piano concerto. Sara smiled. *Mother's happy*, she thought.

Mandy whirled from couch, to window, to chair, improvising her own dance steps. She danced toward her sister without missing a beat and threw her arms around her.

"Mother's going to be working at the bridal shop," she cried. "I get to be your girl!"

Mother stopped playing and swung around on the piano bench. "It's true," she said with a smile. "I start next week."

"I'm glad," Sara replied.

"There's chicken and a baked potato in the micro-wave," Mother said.

"Oh, I should have called," Sara apologized. "I ate at work."

She wandered into the kitchen anyway. A glass of milk would taste good. Mandy followed her. She gyrated around the counter which jutted into the room. Then she spun in an odd pirouette, right in the center of the kitchen, banging her foot into a cabinet.

"Careful, Mandy," Sara cautioned. She offered Mandy a glass of milk and they sat down together on the counter stools.

"I get to be your girl. I get to be your girl," Mandy chanted.

"Hush," Sara admonished. "You'll make Mother feel bad."

A pained expression crossed Mandy's face. "Oh," she said. "I didn't think—" Her mouth twisted in consternation. She jumped up, and raced into the living room, leaving her milk behind.

"She's a tender little kid," Sara mused. She finished her own milk, told her mother and sister good night, and went upstairs. The evening was young, but she felt suddenly weary. She folded back the bedspread and began to undress.

After crawling into bed, she opened her Bible. She only read a few verses from John 14. "Peace I leave with you; My peace I give to you; not as the world gives, do I give to you. Let not your heart be troubled, nor let it be fearful.

"You heard that I said to you, 'I go away, and I will come to you. . . .'"

She turned out the light. The darkness closed around her, heavy and oppressing. She got up and went to the window, releasing the shade and opening the window wide. The air swept in, warm and sweet, full of flower scent and the tang of bruised sage. She smiled. *Dad and his green thumb.*

She lay awake a long time listening to a pair of frogs from the neighbor's pond croaking to one another. *They must be mother and son*, Sara decided. The mother would call in her great deep voice "Come here—come here—come here."

The son's tiny voice creaked back, "Right now—right now—right now."

He evidently didn't mind his mother, his voice never grew weary of answering. They were still calling to one another when Sara fell asleep.

Suddenly, the sound of hurrying footsteps wakened her. For a moment she couldn't put it together. How long had she been asleep? Was someone still up?

She turned onto her side. The red numbers on her clock radio shone 3:47. The frog voices were silent.

Her father's distinct, deep voice drifted up to her room, although his words were unintelligible. It didn't come from her parents' room either. Quite obviously, her parents were moving around. But why?

Sara jumped out of bed and reached for her robe. Its long blue folds settled around her. She sped down the stairs.

Mother stood in the open doorway of the living room, unbelief painted on her pale, strained face. She gestured wordlessly toward the dining room.

Sara brushed past her. Her father looked up from the telephone, a frenzied expression in his eyes. "Police? Yes. We've just been burglarized. I think someone came in through the window."

Sara followed the direction of his look and ran toward it. She pushed the drapes aside and leaned far out into the night.

"Sara!" her mother cried. "Get back!"

Sara scarcely heard her. An unseen car motor throbbed. Then the sound faded, swallowed up in the distant noise of the freeway.

She pulled her head inside and turned to her mother. "Was anything taken?"

"The small stereo in the dining room." Mother's voice wavered. "The drawers in the buffet were left open, too. We haven't been able to determine if anything else is gone."

Sara ran into the dining room and stopped short. The

havoc was incredible: drawers were crazily askew, papers drifted onto the floor.

"How could we have slept through this!" Sara cried. She flew into the kitchen. Even there, drawers and cabinets remained open.

"Great-grandmother's vase!" Mother cried. "It's gone!"

Sara looked at the windowsill where the antique vase had long stood, catching the sun's rays, turning the cut glass a mysterious violet flushed with pink.

"Don't touch anything," her father warned. He put his arm around Mother. "I'm sorry about your vase, honey. I wish . . ."

They wandered through the house. "I just don't understand," Mother kept repeating. "It isn't right."

While her parents were preoccupied, Sara slipped downstairs. Her fingers trembled as she turned on the basement light, but the tunnel door was securely locked. She tiptoed across the cement floor. The key wobbled as Sara placed it in the lock, and she wondered what she expected to find—more running footsteps, someone lurking in the shadows?

She pushed the door open and peered down the tunnel into the empty street. The air seemed oppressive, and even the ivy failed to wave a tendril. The waiting hush of approaching dawn pressed around her.

A car stopped by the entrance and Sara moved forward. Lights illumined the interior of a police car. Sara swallowed hard as she recognized the officer who had questioned her the night of Matt's accident.

"I should tell him about those running footsteps the other night—and the camera," she whispered. "They might think it's important, even though Matt said they probably wouldn't."

Quite suddenly the frog pair resumed their croaking. "Come here—come here." "Right now—right now."

To Sara it was almost a prayer. "Come here, Lord," she murmured, "right now. I need you."

She turned and went back inside.

6 / The Coming of Boris

Sara's entrance couldn't have been better planned if she'd stood outside the basement door and waited for a cue.

The broad-shouldered policeman and her parents looked up as she came into the kitchen. The policeman nodded his head in greeting. "I was just asking your folks if you'd seen anything of Boyd, or picked up any information."

Sara licked her lips. "You mean about the accident?"

Officer Peterson leaned forward, his blue eyes flashing concern.

She took a deep breath. "Are you connecting that with this—?" She gestured around the the disheveled room.

"Are *you*?" he asked.

"I—I'm beginning to wonder—" She looked at her father, an unspoken appeal in her eye. "Dad . . ."

Dad reached for Mother's arm. "Let's leave Sara alone to talk to the officer." He turned to the policeman. "If you have any more questions—"

The policeman stuck out his hand. "We'll be in touch."

Sara saw her parents exchange a look as they left the room. Officer Peterson smiled at her and pulled out a chair.

Sara sat down feeling awkward. She'd changed into jeans and a sailor blouse. Her fingers went to her wide, white collar, nervously creasing and uncreasing its edges.

Her words came out in a rush. She told him all about the camera she'd found at the accident scene, the blond fellow who, after apparently looking for something, had stopped and stared at their house with a menacing gaze. She also mentioned Boyd's recent absence from the drive-in, although he'd been frequenting it for weeks.

"Did you ask the customers he used to hang around with if they'd seen him?"

Sara shook her head. "He wasn't that sort of person. In a way he was a loner. I don't think I ever saw him with anyone."

Officer Peterson slung himself into the chair facing her, his square forehead wrinkling in concentration. "Anything else?"

"Just that the other night—when we heard the prowler—I went downstairs. The door to the tunnel was wide open, and I heard running footsteps. I didn't see anything—except this." Her fingers slid beneath the silver butterfly at her throat. "I lost it the night of Matt's accident."

"Could you have dropped it before you went up the hill?"

"No, I searched everywhere, and so did my little sister. It wasn't there when we retraced my footsteps."

Officer Peterson put his chin into his cupped hand, hunching his shoulders forward. "Sara," he said, "in some ways it hangs together, and in others it doesn't. About the camera—"

"The camera's upstairs in my room, but I gave the film to Matt when he was in the hospital. We thought we might find a clue if we developed it."

"And have you?"

"Developed the film? Not yet. We're planning to to-morrow."

Officer Peterson's fingers drummed restlessly on the table. "Make two copies, will you? I want to see those photos myself." He stood. "I appreciate your cooperation, Sara. And listen, don't lie awake nights worrying about that bur-glar. We'll keep a close watch on you."

A warm glow swept over Sara. "I won't," she said. "And I'll have the pictures for you tomorrow—no, wait. Matt said they'd have to dry overnight."

Officer Peterson nodded. "Day after tomorrow. I'll come by."

They walked to the door. The policeman hesitated an

instant before opening it. "Sara," he said, "don't be afraid to confide in your parents. They're good eggs." His hand raised in a quick farewell; then he was gone.

Carefully, Sara locked the door. She went back upstairs but not to sleep. Her thoughts whirled helplessly, sucking her into a well of weary confusion.

That night the dream came again. It was a dream she had had many times before, as far back as she could remember. Sometimes variations colored the details, but it was always basically the same.

Something dreadful happened in her dream, and Sara was never quite sure what it was. But she knew she must telephone for help.

Her heart would pound furiously and her hands tremble as she dialed. And then a voice— "I'm sorry. Your call cannot be completed as dialed. Please check the number and dial again or ask your operator for assistance."

She would slam down the receiver, lift it, and dial again. Nothing—no tone—nothing.

She would try again. This time a busy signal—buzzing—buzzing—buzzing.

Sara wakened. Her heart thudded. A dream. It had only been a dream. But this time something unusual nibbled at her consciousness. She frowned, trying to grab hold of the elusive difference, wondering why it seemed so important.

Mandy—she'd been alone with Mandy. And something horrible had happened—

Sara jumped out of bed and hurried to her sister's room. Mandy slept peacefully, her arms circled over her head, one bare foot sticking out from the bedding.

Sara pulled the blanket over the protruding foot, and Mandy stirred. "Mamma," she murmured, "Mamma—" A sleepy smile slid across her face, and she turned onto her side.

Sara bent and lightly kissed her cheek. She returned to her room, curiously peaceful. The sight of her little sister had somehow banished the dream. She could sleep now.

Morning light spangled the breakfast table with gold

squares and dazzled a fistful of dandelions that Mandy had shoved into a miniature vase.

Sara's father sat alone, hunched over a steaming cup of black coffee. The lines in his brow deepened as she seated herself opposite him. "Sara," he said, "I don't want you to quit your job at the Burgermill."

Sara started to open her lips, but he silenced her with a sweeping gesture. "That havoc last night—I can't have two girls staying alone—even in daylight."

Sara glanced around the room. "How did you get it straightened up so quickly?"

Dad rubbed the dark stubble on his chin. "Your mother and I worked for quite a while after you went upstairs. And Sara, I'd rather you said nothing to Mandy. I hate to put fear in her."

Sara nodded. "But she'll wonder, Dad. She was all excited yesterday when she told me about Mother's job and my staying with her."

Her father sighed. "I know. She'll just have to attribute it to the peculiarities of adults. I'm sorry, honey."

"It's all right," Sara replied. She picked up a neatly-folded cloth napkin and toyed with the edges. "Dad, would it seem right to you if I left my job anyway, even if I wasn't needed to help with Mandy?"

"We talked about that earlier, Sara. Jobs aren't that plentiful now."

"I know. But if I just stay home—"

"What would you do with your time, Sara? Most of your friends are away or working. Idleness can be just as harmful as working in the wrong job."

"I could learn a craft. Your grandmother made samplers. Maybe I could, too. Besides, Dad, I'm a little bit afraid."

Her troubled gray eyes met his steady ones. "I can't help but feel there's some connection between Boyd—and the hit-and-run driver—and the intruder we had last night." She gestured around the room.

"Did you tell the police?"

Sara nodded. "He said he'd keep an eye on the house. But he can't watch the drive-in or follow my bus around."

"Are you sure you're not magnifying things? Putting together the wrong pieces?"

"I don't know." She stared down at the table, then changed the subject abruptly. "I went to see Matt when he was in the hospital. He came over to the Burgermill last night."

"And?" her father probed.

"He asked if he could take me out to his house tomorrow and show me his dark room." Quickly she told him about the camera she'd found the morning after the accident. "Officer Peterson agrees we might find a clue in the film. Matt and I would like to develop the roll together."

Mr. Faulkner sighed deeply. "What kind of boy is he, Sara? He looked like a nice person but—"

"I don't know him very well," Sara confessed. "But he seems different. We even talk about God."

Her father's fingers traced around the top of his coffee cup. "Sara, I appreciate your asking me about this. When I found out about your interest in Boyd, I was disappointed and angry. Deep inside I felt we'd failed each other. I even determined it would be a long time before I'd let you date again—even boys from church."

He reached out and touched her hand. "I know you've felt that I've been watching you—and I have. Once someone lets me down, I have a hard time trusting him again. I keep thinking, 'let him prove himself.' But Sara, I've noticed a change in your attitude. It's been good."

A loving warmth slid into the corners of Sara's heart, banishing the dark shadows lurking there. The silence trembled between them.

"It isn't really a date," she said after a while. "In fact, if you said that to Matt, I think it would scare him to death!"

She pursued the subject thoughtfully. "I get the impression that girls don't mean much to him aside from friends. He's all wrapped up in wanting to know who God is, and about birds—"

"And motorcycles and film developing?"

Sara grinned. "You said it!"

Her father stood up abruptly. "Go ahead and go with him, Sara," he said with quick decision. "Maybe it's an answer to prayer."

He strode out of the room, and Sara sat still, her mood spiraling to meet the gold dandelions, the warm sunshine. Her dad was starting to trust her again. That, too, was an answer to prayer.

Quite suddenly, Sara bowed her head. "Lord," she whispered, "if you want me to keep working at the drive-in, you'll have to give me strength. But, Lord, it seems like Mother needs a change right now. Would you show Dad that Mandy and I will be safe together here alone?"

The answer to Sara's prayer came from a totally unexpected source. Her shift at the Burgermill had been busy and uneventful—no sign of Boyd, nor Hot and Sweet. Even Doreen and Lonnie were quieter than usual.

Back home, when Sara stepped onto the porch, a movement in the window caught her eye. A huge brown dog looked out at her, its mouth wide, opened in a distinct smile framing big, white teeth.

The front door burst open and a very animated Mandy dashed through it.

"It's Boris!" Mandy cried. "He's a dog, and he's come to live with us to be our protector!"

The head vanished from the window and reappeared at Mandy's shoulder. "Why, he's as big as a—a pony!" Sara gasped. "Whatever will we do with him?"

The dark hulk advanced toward her, his long tail wagging. "I've never seen such a huge dog. What kind is it anyway? Where did he come from?"

"He's a Great Dane! And would you believe it? He weighs 175 pounds! Dad and I went across town after Daddy got off work and brought him home in the car."

Mandy giggled. "He sure looked funny. Daddy wanted to call him Samuel, but the man who owned him said, 'Please, call him Boris.' "

"Samuel? Why Samuel?"

"Because it means 'asked of the Lord.' Daddy had asked, you see—" She raised her eyebrows, twisting her mouth into a rosebud. "He told me about the burglar last night. He said he wasn't going to at first, then changed his mind."

Sara nodded. She looked at the dog thoughtfully. "He's such a huge beast he could easily handle three names. How about Samuel Boris Faulkner?"

Mandy looked doubtful. "Sam doesn't suit him. And the man who raised him asked us to call him Boris."

Mother joined them on the porch. Sara looked at her closely. Last night's upheaval didn't seem to affect her spirit. Her soft brown hair was smoothed to perfection and her eyes shone with blue lights.

"He certainly is big, isn't he!" Mother appeared to be trying to get used to the idea.

"What does he eat?" Sara asked.

"Dad says just dog food," Mandy replied.

Sara reached out a tentative hand. "I wish I were a little bit smaller," she complained. "I could hop on his back and ride. Why is he wearing a studded collar?" She touched it curiously, fascinated by the bristling stainless steel spikes. Her hand moved upward. The dog's forehead was smooth beneath her exploring fingertips.

"He's very gentle," Mother said. "The collar helps make him seem more—more formidable to intruders." She turned to Mandy. "Run inside and get a handful of dog food, honey. He's cute when he eats."

Mandy hurried out, and her mother spoke softly to Sara. "He's an answer to prayer," she confided. "This morning your father said, 'No way am I going to let Sara stay home alone with Mandy, even in daylight. Not with the furor we've been having.' " Mother ran her hand over Boris's back. "And then at work he saw an ad on the bulletin board. It just hit him all at once—a great big watch dog. And with me in the position of wanting to say yes for the first time in my life about a dog—well, he jumped at the chance."

Sara's gray eyes softened. "He is an answer to prayer,"

she mused, "for both of us." *But what an ugly one*, she thought.

Mandy ran out onto the porch. She held out a food-filled palm to the dog, and Sara watched with awe as the huge jaws crunched the hard biscuits with ease.

"I'd like a picture of that," she told her mother.

"Why not?" Mother asked. She vanished into the house.

Boris crunched in the silence. Mandy started to give him another biscuit, but Sara stopped her.

"Mother's getting the camera," she said. "We want a picture of you feeding him."

A sudden cry caused both girls to race to the kitchen. Mother stood in front of an open drawer.

"My camera!" she cried. "It was there in the drawer with my film. They're both gone. Gone!"

She wrung her hands. "They even stole the roll I'd already taken." She stared at the startled girls. "I don't understand it. I just don't understand!"

7 / Clues from the Dark Room

"I'm sure now. The camera we found must have belonged to the man who knocked you down," Sara told Matt, concluding her narration of the preceding day's events. "Otherwise, why would he break in and take Mother's camera?" She waited for his reaction.

Matt nodded thoughtfully. The fingers of his unbandaged hand tightened on the steering wheel.

"It sure sounds like it," he agreed. "We'll soon find out. Whoever took those pictures must know there's something there that will identify him."

Sara sighed and leaned back in the seat. A curious calm spread through her. *God must be working*, she thought, *otherwise I'd be falling apart, piece by piece*.

She glanced at Matt. A slight frown wrinkled his forehead. Then he turned to her, his quick smile contrasting white, even teeth and tanned face.

"Everything's ready to go at home, but I need your help." He inclined his head toward his damaged hand. "I can't get the roll into the container without using both hands. You'll have to do it."

"If I can," Sara said doubtfully.

"You'll be able to do it easily. I'll show you how. You can practice on an old roll first." Matt paused. "Sara, about your job—how's it going? Did you decide to look for another?"

"Not exactly. I've already talked to my parents. We've decided to do something different."

"Different?" Matt prodded.

"Mother wants me to stay home this summer and watch Mandy. At first I wasn't particularly enthused—" Sudden animation tinged her voice. "But now I'm getting excited. I mean, well—I guess it's because I really think it's what the Lord wants." Her long lashes whisked up. "Matt, do you think I'm on the right track?"

"About your staying home or about clues on the film?"

"Both."

Matt grinned. "You're on the right track, Sara—on both counts. And somehow I think that the Lord, who knows all things, is directing your thinking." He drove the car into a long driveway. "Well, Sara, this is my home."

Sara looked around eagerly. Tall, young firs still tasseled in spring green fringed the roadway. Just ahead, a brown house snuggled into a patch of green lawn bordered with stately purple foxgloves and yellow irises. A narrow cement path guided them into a small clematis-draped porch.

"It's beautiful, Matt!" Sara exclaimed. "Someone in your family must have a green thumb."

"Mother does," he announced proudly. "All spring long she digs in her flower beds, shapes the bushes—"

A woman with a sweet smile opened the door. She had soft, brown hair, and wore a plaid blouse and jeans. Immediately Sara felt at home.

"Sara," Matt's mother said, "I'm so glad you've come."

"I'm happy to be here," Sara responded.

Matt started to show her the darkroom, but his mother delayed them. "First, come and have some milk and cookies," she suggested. "They're fresh from the oven and oh, so good."

Matt didn't need urging. He poured three glasses of milk, and they all sat down around the table, munching cookies, laughing, and chatting.

Mrs. Roberts was full of questions. What school did Sara go to? Had she ever lived in the country? Did her church have a good youth program?

Sara enjoyed the conversation and the company, but she was eager to see that film.

When the cookies were gone, Matt and Sara went to the darkroom. Golden cream wallpaper with an eagle design attested that this once had been a small bedroom. Little evidence remained. A counter with a small sink lined the far wall. In the middle of the room stood a large table, cluttered with film paraphernalia.

But Sara's eyes were drawn to the bold, black and white photos that decorated one wall. She stepped toward them. A small dragonfly rested on a large leaf. A bumble bee hovered above a foxglove; water skippers poised on the surface of a creek. Sara almost felt a breeze touch her cheek, almost saw the water quicken and flow beneath the skippers' darting feet.

Matt's shoulder moved close to her own. "Do you like them?"

"Love them! Makes me wish I could—"

"You can." He picked up a roll of undeveloped black and white film and pressed it into her hand. "When we get back to your house remind me, and I'll show you how to load our lost-and-found camera."

Sara slipped the film into her pocket. "You must enjoy photographing small things," she observed.

"Sometimes." He took her hand and pulled her toward another display on the opposite wall. Sara caught a quick breath. The enlarged color photographs drew her like a magnet: a sunset in shades of gold and peach above a quiet bay, mallards outlined against towering thunderheads, a canoe reflected in a stream with a lone duck poised on the prow.

"These are my experiments with color. But I don't develop it yet. Too expensive. As you can see," he explained, "wildlife is my thing. I'm happiest when I'm hiking, camping, living off the land—"

"And learning about God," Sara interrupted.

He nodded. "Yes, I have to admit I feel cheated if I can't get up early in the morning and have my quiet time in the woods." He pointed to a photo of a moss-covered stump.

"That's where I meet the Lord," he confided. "It's so beautiful. A stream runs below. That's where I photographed those water skippers there."

"What do you do if it rains? Do you still have your quiet time?"

"Well," he confessed, "I just pull my blankets up higher under my chin and roll over." He shook his head. "Not really. Only sometimes. Most of the time I get up and open my window and my Bible."

He turned to the table covered with a disorderly array of developing tanks, thermometers and empty film cartridges. He picked up one of them and handed it to her.

"Just take this"—he gave her a roll of old film—"and thread it in like so."

Sara's fingers fumbled. "You mean I have to do this in the dark?"

"Just do it several times. You'll catch on," Matt assured her.

Sara gained confidence as she threaded and rethreaded the film. Matt handed her the other film and turned out the light.

Sara felt a moment of apprehension. "What if I ruin it?"

"You won't. Just do like I said."

Sara's fingers steadied. The film slid into the reel, and she tightened the lid. "I did it!" she exclaimed.

Matt turned on the light and grinned at her. "Nothing to it," he said. "All I have to do is develop it, then hang the negatives up to dry."

Sara stood beside him in front of the sink, her anticipation mounting. Matt explained each step as he worked. Her fascination increased as she watched Matt agitate the chemicals with a watchful eye on the clock.

But when Sara clipped the negative strips up to dry, disappointment surged through her. "There aren't any faces here at all, just cars. All kinds of them."

They peered at the negatives together, Matt's face reflecting Sara's own discouragement. "Maybe when they're printed, we'll be able to pick up a license plate number," he muttered.

Sara squinted, tiny lines crinkling around her steady gray eyes. "Matt," she said, "there's one here of a house, an unusual house."

Matt's eyes followed her pointing finger. "You're right,"

he said. "It looks like it was built around the turn of the century, like the ones you see in the older sections of Portland."

"Portland is so big," she said doubtfully. "I wonder what our chances would be of finding it."

She peered again at the wet negatives. Something niggled at the back of her mind, but she couldn't figure it out. Was it the house? Had she seen it before? Or was it something about the cars?

Matt picked up a lamp and shone it directly on the strips, searching for details. "I wish I had a negative drier," he said suddenly. "We could print these up in just a few hours." He moved the lamp back to its former position. "We'll have to wait until morning, Sara. I'll do them up first thing and bring them to you. I hope—" His voice dwindled into silence as he took her arm and steered her out the door and back to the kitchen.

Matt's mother waited eagerly in front of the stove, a spatula in her hand. "Nothing," Matt said. "Just cars, cars, cars—all different."

"And one picture of a house," Sara interjected. "But no faces. I was hoping we'd have something special to show that policeman."

"Ah, well," Mrs. Roberts soothed, "you tried. Oh, Sara, before I forget, I have your white sweater. Let me get it for you." She disappeared only to return quickly with a white reminder of the night of the accident. "I soaked it in cold water and the bloodstains came right out," she said proudly.

"Thank you," Sara replied, draping the sweater over her arm. "I almost forgot about it myself.—Wait," she said suddenly. "That one car, Matt, could I have another look?"

They hurried back to the drying negatives. Sara examined them carefully. "Look at the third one down," she urged; "it looks familiar."

Matt seemed unimpressed. "Working where you work, they could *all* look familiar."

Sara didn't answer. "It's a Chevrolet. I'll bet it's dark

green," she said triumphantly. "And I know who drives it: Hot and Sweet." She brushed its fender lightly with the tip of her finger. "You wait. When you get your prints done, you'll find a dent right there. And here in the corner of the windshield will be a crack. It'll be barely discernible, but if you'll look closely, you'll see it."

She was unprepared for Matt's response. His good arm clasped her tightly around the waist as he swung her into a circle. Jubilance rang in her ears. "Maybe we do have a clue after all. You wonderful girl, you. I didn't know I had a female Sherlock Holmes on my hands."

Sara laughed. "I only hope I'm right," she said breathlessly. "But it's something, it really is!"

That night Sara turned restlessly in her bed, her mind seething with questions. Did Hot and Sweet really fit into the accident and the intrusion of their home? Was there a connection between him and Boyd? And what about the mysterious blond fellow?

She looked at the red numbers on her clock. A sinking sensation rolled inside her. It was 11:30. Dad had called it "prime time for excitement around here."

"I'm being silly," she whispered. She pulled her blanket up under her chin, but her uneasiness persisted. Tossing her covers off, she walked barefoot to the window.

The dark bulk of the rhododendrons and ivy was still, the street empty in the night. Sara's frog friends croaked their repetitive messages, and she smiled.

"Come here, come here."

"Right now, right now, right now."

Sara stiffened, aware of a tense electricity in the air. Her questing gray eyes probed the night.

A police car cruised down the darkened street. It slowed in front of the house, speeded up, and was gone.

Sara remained motionless, her thoughts darting like birds searching for insects. The hedge branches stirred, and a large dark shape moved onto the sidewalk.

Sara's hands trembled as she gripped the window ledge. She leaned forward, peering into the darkness.

It wasn't human. Her mouth dried, and she licked her lips. A sudden muffled laugh rose above the pounding of her heart. Boris?

Sara rushed from her room and flew down the steps, her nightgown trailing in the darkness. She stepped onto the porch calling softly, "Boris! Boris!"

He came toward her from the shadows of the great oak guarding the street, his big tongue lolling, his tail wagging. "You silly creature," Sara chided as he came close. Affection stirred inside her as she put both hands on his huge forehead.

"You're supposed to be watching out for us, not wandering into the street. What happened anyway? Did someone leave the gate unlatched?"

Sara looked down at her gown. "I'm not going out like this, Boris. Come inside." She opened the door wide and Boris followed her.

"You can sleep in here and risk Mother's wrath," she said, gesturing at the floor. "Make yourself comfortable."

Boris wasn't interested. He tucked his great muzzle into Sara's hand and looked entreatingly into her eyes.

Sara shrugged her shoulders and started up the stairs. Boris followed, his paws thudding on the steps.

At the door to her room she turned. "If you come in, you'll have to be a gentleman," she admonished. "You'll have to treat my Garfield right."

Boris seemed to understand. In dignified silence he stalked in and lay down on the floor at the foot of the bed.

He put his massive head on his outstretched paws and regarded her unblinkingly. Sara smiled at her hulking companion, then crawled into bed. As she turned out the light, the frogs started a new question. "You here? You here? You here?"

Boris's breathing mingled with their croaks and Sara's eyes grew heavy. She could sleep now.

8 / Mystery Car

Matt laid the photos on the Faulkners' dining room table and stood back. "I'm sorry, Sara," he said. "There isn't much. No license plate number, no cracked windshield—nothing but that dented fender."

Sara peered at the photo beneath his finger. "You're right," she agreed. "The crack doesn't show at all."

"It's a common enough place for a car to have a dented fender," Matt reminded her.

The eagerness that had swelled so quickly inside Sara when Matt stepped onto her front porch dipped low. "It's probably just coincidence," she said softly. "But Officer Peterson is picking up the extra set of prints this afternoon anyway. Maybe he'll find something."

They stared at the photos in silence. "I have a surprise in the car for our lunch," Matt said after a while. "I'll go get it."

"Oh, Matt, you needn't have. When I asked you over yesterday I didn't expect—"

Matt grinned and leaned forward. One finger came up and tapped her lightly on the nose. "Shh."

"But Mother has pizza in the fridge. All we have to do is heat, eat, and enjoy. And if I know Mom, she'll come in any moment with store-bought cookies."

Matt's grin deepened into mystery. "This isn't store-bought," he said. "All you have to do is promise to eat."

Sara selected a photograph from the table and pretended to study it intently. "Well—" she challenged.

"Promise? To eat it? I fixed it myself."

"Of course. Now go get it before I die an unnatural death."

71

Matt laughed and hurried out the door. His "Remember, you promised" drifted back to the dining room.

Sara smiled, then bent over the photos. She couldn't believe the Chevrolet wasn't Hot and Sweet's. But of course she couldn't prove it—not without the revealing cracks in the windshield.

She looked again at the fascinating old house. Its turrets and rounded windows lent a peculiar old-time charm.

"I have half a notion to go searching for you, house beautiful," she mused.

The door opened and in came Mandy and Mother, carrying groceries. "Ooh, pictures!" Mandy squealed. "Let me see."

"They aren't ours," Sara explained. "They belong to Matt—or rather the camera I found." She picked up the house photo and handed it to her mother. "Have you seen this house before?"

Her mother frowned over the top of her brown paper bag. "No, not that I know of."

"We bought cookies, Sara," Mandy interrupted. "Yummy oatmeal and chocolate chip."

Matt stepped into the room, holding a glass bowl in his hand.

"And Grandma's molasses bars," Sara finished for her. She winked at Matt and he winked back, holding the bowl out to her.

She looked at its contents curiously. "What is it, Matt?"

Mandy and Mother crowded around eagerly.

"It's a wild salad that I gathered this morning," he explained. "It's a little late in the season, but I found Miner's lettuce, yellow violet leaves—we call them Johnny-jump-ups—"

Mandy touched a thin elongated leaf. "Is this a dandelion leaf?"

Matt looked at her approvingly. "It sure is. If it were a bit earlier in the season, I'd have put in fern fiddle heads. They're good."

"What do they taste like?" Sara asked.

"Um, a little like a raw green bean—only stronger. You'd have to taste one yourself to really know."

"Am I supposed to serve this wild thing?" Mother asked dubiously.

Matt laughed, a clear, ringing laugh that seemed to have some of the sparkle of a mountain stream. "Sure," he answered. "It's good as is, or you can add a bit of dressing. Italian tastes great on it."

Mother shook her head as she opened the refrigerator. "Dandelions, Miner's lettuce—" Removing a large pizza from the shelf, she set it on the counter and laughed. "What a combination—junk food and wild delicacies."

"Pizza's not junk food," Sara retorted; "it has lots of good, high-quality protein, tomatoes—"

"And sausage and olives and cheese," Mandy chimed in. "Hurry up, Mom. I'm starved."

Matt and Sara set the table with red-checked napkins and plain white plates, while Mother and Mandy scurried around the kitchen, readying lunch.

Sara stepped back from the table, smiling approval at its cheery appearance. "Your salad looks pretty enough to be a centerpiece, Matt."

Matt cocked his head to one side. "It sure does."

"No," Mandy protested. "We need flowers." She dove for the drawer which held the garden shears, and brandished them in the air. "Matt and I will get them."

"Oh, no, you won't," Mother intercepted. "You're helping me." She handed the shears to Sara. "Would you? Dad's garden is flourishing and it's a shame to keep it all outside."

Sara nodded and took the shears. "I'll go with you," Matt volunteered.

The two tripped gaily down the stairs and into the side yard. A soft breeze ruffled their hair and brought the sweet scent of honeysuckle to their noses. Matt sniffed and looked around appreciatively.

Red and white roses spilled over the fence, vying with the prolific grape vine for a place of importance. The beds in front sported a glorious profusion of deep blue delphiniums and red and white snapdragons.

"That's it!" Matt cried. "A bit of blue—"

"And red and white," Sara finished for him. She stepped to the edge of the lawn and selected several long-stemmed snapdragons and single tall delphinium. For a moment she peered into its white-starred center.

"I'd like to draw it," she said, "just the way it is."

Matt's eyebrows darted up. "You draw?"

A slight flush tinted Sara's cheeks. "Just simple things really—like leaves, mushrooms. I'm not much good."

"I'd like to see them, Sara. You might be surprised."

Sara nodded, then abruptly changed the subject. "About the cars, Matt. What do you think they mean?"

Matt shook his head. "I don't know. Maybe whoever took the pictures has a weird hobby."

The window above their heads slid open. "Pizza's ready. We'll give you five minutes," Mandy called. She hung out the window, her long blond hair dangling, a mischievous smile lighting her elfin face.

Little pest, Sara thought. "We'll be right there," she called, starting up the porch steps.

Matt stopped her. "Your tunnel," he said. "I'd like to see it."

Sara turned, confusion tangling her thoughts. "Why?"

Matt shrugged. "Just curious. I happen to like tunnels."

Sara's eyebrows drew together in a question.

Matt laughed. "I have a tunnel," he explained. "It's in the woods and it's beautiful. It must have been a road once, but now it's overgrown with all kinds of things—honeysuckle, wild roses. The clematis and vine maple mingle and droop down, making green and gold shadows. Wild things hide there. Birds, butterflies, chipmunks—"

"Our tunnel isn't like that at all, Matt," Sara interrupted. "Our house is old. We don't use the tunnel now, but at one time it was the service entrance to the street.

She sighed and shook her head. "It's ugly, Matt. Just old gray cement."

"And ivy," Matt said. "I've seen it waving around the opening."

"Sara! Matt!" Mandy called.

"Coming!" Sara shouted. Her fingers tightened around her flowers as they hurried up the steps and into the house.

The bright bouquet, coupled with the tangy wild salad, made lunch a gala occasion. *Or was it Matt's company?* Sara wondered. He was different. Something in his personality drew her like a magnet—not the way Boyd had. This was something equally exciting, and somehow better.

After lunch Sara and Matt walked out to Matt's pickup. "I appreciate your taking me to work," she said as she got in and set her purse on the dented floorboards.

"It's my last day, you know," she confided. "Mother begins her job at the bridal shop next week."

"Glad?"

Sara frowned thoughtfully. "Yes, I am. I really feel it's what the Lord wants." She twisted her collar. "I want to start a quiet time, too, Matt. Ever since I saw that picture of your green, mossy stump, I've felt a yearning inside."

Matt flashed a huge grin. "It's the best thing that's ever happened to me," he said. "Somehow when I take the time to read my Bible and learn to think His thoughts, it's transforming. My whole day has more purpose. Except sometimes I think the pressures are greater."

"What do you mean?"

"Our youth pastor explained it rather well I think. He said that Satan becomes more active when he sees us giving God first place. Pastor Dale shared a verse that really encouraged me, though. It's 'Greater is He who is in you than he who is in the world.' "

Sara rummaged through her purse for a pencil. "Where do you find that?" she asked, pulling out a stubby pencil and small note pad. "I might begin my own quiet time there."

"First John 4:4," he said, glancing sideways. The clump of flowers decorating the note paper's edge caught his attention. "Did you draw that?"

Sara covered her sketch in a quick gesture.

"But it's lovely," Matt protested. "Please, could I see it?"

Sara uncovered the paper reluctantly. "It's just something I play around with."

"Wild Camas," he exclaimed, "and you a city girl."

"Lots of wild things grow in the woods along Terwilliger Boulevard," Sara said. "I go there a lot. Sometimes with Mandy, sometimes alone."

"Any mossy stumps available?" Matt teased.

"I wasn't thinking *that* especially. But maybe it is a good idea—a quiet place away from the house."

Matt nodded. "The place isn't too important, though," he said. "It's taking the time to be with God that makes the difference—and doing it daily. For me that means setting a time."

Sara looked up. "Which is?"

"Nine in the morning, right now. I'm working afternoons and evenings."

"Nine o'clock," Sara mused. "I wonder—"

Matt grinned. "Want to join me? That's how my friend, Russ, and I helped each other get going. We were separated by miles but our spirits touched."

Sara nodded. She put her note pad inside her purse and looked at him. His tanned hands gripped the wheel. A light-blue shirt, open at the neck, exposed his tanned neck. His brown hair swirled in soft waves around his face.

He's good-looking enough to be one of those outdoorsmen in the commercials, she thought. Then he turned, and the vulnerability and gentleness around his mouth banished her illusion. *He knows his God,* she thought, *I wish I did—*

The drive-in was already a flurry of activity when Matt dropped Sara off a few minutes later. Immediately the rush absorbed her as she wrote orders and collected money.

Customers kept her too busy to think of quiet times, or mossy stumps, or old houses and cracked windshields for that matter.

Toward evening, she looked out the window and saw the familiar green Chevrolet. Hot and Sweet's gaze caught hers at once. He closed one eye in a long, suggestive wink.

Sara's heart jumped and fluttered in her throat. To distract herself, she looked at the windshield, then at the dented fender. Neither defect was visible.

She clasped her hands together and turned from the window. Her chin lifted with quick courage as she opened the door and walked to the car.

Hot and Sweet watched her with a dark glint in his eye. "Aha, sweetheart," he said as she came closer. "Miss High Hat's down from her pedestal."

"Not really," Sara said quietly. "I just wanted to ask you something."

"Ask on. I'm at your command."

His look was intense. Sara held her ground. She reached out and touched the windshield. "What happened to the crack?" she asked.

The smile faded from Hot and Sweet's face. Something dark and formidable touched his eyes. "Never was a crack," he said. "What made you think there was?"

Sara tossed her head in unbelief. "There was," she said. "And I don't see why you should deny it. And the fender—" she pursued. "The dent is gone."

The scowl on Hot and Sweet's face deepened. "You're imagining things," he said brusquely, "mixing my car up with another."

"I'm not," Sara persisted. "How long have you been driving it, anyway?"

Hot and Sweet's hand shot out and clasped her wrist.

"Let me go!" Sara cried.

"Not unless you tell me what you're getting at," he hissed.

Sara felt her heart plunge from her throat into her stomach. For a moment she thought she would lose her lunch. Memory of a mossy-green stump, of Matt saying, "Greater is He that is in you," flashed through her mind. Courage returned. Her thoughts stilled, and she remembered something. *Dad's been looking for someone to take out the dents in our back fender.*

She smiled sweetly at the angry man. "I was wondering where you got your body work done. My father is looking for somebody reliable to do work on our car." She waved her free hand airily.

His scowl deepened, and he tighted the grasp on her wrist.

Doubt mingled with her unanswered questions. What *was* she getting at anyway?

"Ah," she murmured, "now I'm wondering—perhaps it was another green Chevrolet, same year, but the color could have been darker—"

The clasping fingers released her. His angry look seemed to fade as he looked at her. "How'd you like to go for a ride?" he tempted. "We could run up to the restaurant on Skyline Boulevard. Have a Coke—"

Sara smiled gently. "Other plans," she replied. "So sorry." She started to turn away but Hot and Sweet stopped her.

"My order," he protested.

A warmth crept into Sara's cheeks. "Sorry."

Hot and Sweet licked his lips. "Make it a hamburger with everything—and coffee." The suggestive lear rose into his eyes and Sara drew back.

She scribbled the order and turned away, almost running for the door. Stopping to take a deep breath, she steadied her heartbeat, then went inside.

Sara turned to the window. The green Chevrolet was backing out of the lot, its movements quick and jerky. Then it was gone, but not before Sara had observed the license plate number. She wrote it on the back of her order pad— AGC 540.

9 / Matt's Pond

Tangled roses clambered over the fence, their white blooms striving to imitate the snowy clouds scattered in the morning sky. Blue delphiniums stretched heavenward, trying to touch their distant Creator.

Like me, Sara thought, *trying to reach out to my Lord*.

She sat on the bench in the side yard, her open Bible on her lap. Boris lay beside her, his huge muzzle resting on her feet, his bright eyes darting from flower to flower.

Boris lifted his head abruptly. Sara turned to follow his gaze.

A robin crouched in the grass, its neck pulled in, wings half-spread like a tiny helpless kite. Sara put her Bible on the bench and walked toward the bird, Boris close behind her.

The bird lifted its head and tensed. Then it beat its wings on the ground and lifted into the air.

"It's her leg, Boris," Sara explained. "See how it dangles?"

They went back to the bench. Sara sat down and picked up her Bible. Boris folded his huge legs beneath him, resuming his former pose.

Absently, Sara reached out and smoothed his muzzle. She looked up at the leaves of the great maple overhead.

"Lord," she murmured, "you seem so far away."

David felt like this, she recalled. *Somewhere in the Psalms he pleaded with the Lord not to be silent, not to be far from him*.

"I'm trying to reach out to God, Boris," she explained. But was she? Her thoughts kept racing to Matt—the photos—to Hot and Sweet's hasty exit the night before.

She shook her head and thoughtfully began turning the pages, picking out a phrase here, a thought there.

Suddenly, the words from Psalm 34 jumped off the page at her, "The Lord is near to the brokenhearted, and saves those who are crushed in spirit."

"Maybe that's what's wrong," she mused. "Perhaps if I'm to have a strong new me inside, I'll have to have a broken and crushed heart first."

The conviction grew within her. True, she was ashamed of the attraction she still felt at times for the handsome Boyd, discouraged with her spiritual life which seemed like a yo-yo. But a broken heart?"

"I never thought of how it looked to you, Lord. I mean I've been sorry, but I never really thought how my sin makes you feel."

Pain stirred inside her. She remembered the story of the ninety and nine sheep and the one little lamb who was lost. The Shepherd searched for the lamb until He found it. She pictured Him gathering the lamb up in His arms, holding it close, then carrying it home on His shoulder.

"Poor, weary, crushed little lamb," she whispered. She underlined the verse in Psalms before she went inside. Her first day with Mandy was about to begin.

The two of them were dawdling over a late breakfast when the phone rang. Excitement tinged Sara's voice as she recognized Matt's deep tones.

"Why, Matt. Anything new?"

"No, but would you and Mandy like to go to the pond with me?"

Sara's heart did a flip-flop, then quietly resumed its usual steady beat. "I'm not sure, Matt. I'd have to call Mom."

"And if she says yes?"

Sara laughed breathlessly. "Of course," she said. "Mandy would love it, too!"

Mandy's blue eyes widened as she looked up over the top of her glass of milk. "Love what?" she demanded.

"An outing at Matt's pond. You'd like it, Mandy."

Mandy set her glass down with a smack that threatened

to shatter it. "To the pond!" she cried. "Now?"

Sara smiled and nodded. "I'll call you back, Matt." She hung up the phone and quickly dialed the bridal shop.

Mandy leaped from her chair and circled her arms around Sara's neck. "Tell her to say yes," she willed. "Please—"

Permission granted, Mandy whirled around the room. "To the pond, to the pond," she chanted. Sara rolled her eyes and dialed Matt's number.

"That's that," she said as she put down the receiver. "Matt will be here in an hour." She looked at her little sister critically. "You'd better change your blouse."

Mandy flew up the stairs two at a time and Sara cleared the table. It would be fun to explore Matt's pond, she decided, but most of all, it would be fun to be with Matt. Maybe she could talk to him about becoming near to God.

She tossed her dishrag into the sink and went upstairs. After she changed into her favorite jeans and blue plaid shirt, she went to the window and looked down at the side yard. She always marveled at the difference a bird's-eye view made. It almost made you want to be one—fly high—

"Mrs. Robin," she exclaimed, "you're back!"

The bird hunched down as she had before. As Sara watched, the robin turned, looked at the ground around her, cocked her head, then stabbed with her beak. An angle worm wriggled to get free.

Sara turned quickly to the drawer where she'd placed the camera. If she could just get a photo to show Matt—

She hurried down the stairs and out into the yard just in time to see the robin flutter a few feet to another spot. The bird stabbed again and another worm dangled in the air. Sara focused carefully and pressed the button. The camera clicked, and elation filled her. She had captured the bird forever on film. This was almost as much fun as drawing flowers.

Sara moved forward, refocusing the lens. But the robin fluttered, took wing, and flew away.

Sara was undaunted. Carefully, she focused on a white-eyed delphinium, then a shadowed rose still shimmery with dew. She was still in the garden when Matt came, Boris and Mandy bounding beside him.

"Aha!" he exclaimed. "I see you've been bitten."

"Your photographs did it," she confessed. "I just hope this thing is set right."

Matt took the camera and examined it. "It's okay. They ought to turn out great." He handed it back to her. "You're on the last picture, though."

Sara gasped. "Already?" she moaned. "I was going to take it to the pond."

"I don't have extra film," Matt apologized. "But my camera's loaded. It's in the pickup."

"I'll leave this one here then," Sara said. "Wait. One last picture—"

She backed Mandy, Matt and Boris against the roses and aimed. Matt laughed, stuck his head close to Mandy's and made a silly face. Sara tried not to giggle as she snapped the picture.

Hurriedly, she took the camera to her room and dumped it in the drawer. Then the three of them were off, packed together in Matt's father's old dilapidated pickup.

Matt didn't bother to apologize for his vehicle. "I'm kind of fond of this old thing," he confessed. "Dad's had it since I was a little kid."

They jounced cheerily down the street and onto the freeway. "It has a hard time keeping up," Matt said.

"I don't mind," Sara replied.

"Neither do I," said Mandy. "It's like an old man. Does it have a name?"

Matt laughed. "Funny you should ask. We call it Doc, after the dwarf in Snow White."

"Doc," Mandy mused, accenting it with her tongue. "Doc."

Sara thought Grumpy would be more appropriate.

As they left Portland behind, Sara told Matt about her encounter with Hot and Sweet. "I got his license plate number, too," she explained, "just in case—"

Matt nodded. "That's good."

In spite of Doc's slow speed they arrived at their destination in good time. They parked alongside the road and got out. Mandy, unable to contain her exuberance, bounded ahead, sailing over deep cow ruts and tufts of grass. Matt sprinted close to her and grabbed her hand.

"Slow down, young'un," he entreated. "If you burst through here like a two-ton truck, you'll scare the wildlife away."

Reluctantly, Mandy slowed her pace to match the more decorous speed of the other two. "Are there really ducks here?" she asked. "And water skippers?"

Matt swung her hand cheerily. "Sure are. And salamanders, too."

"Ugh," Sara groaned. "They're so ugly—"

Matt caught her hand in his, and the three of them walked together. A warmth that rivaled the midday sunshine grew within Sara. She smiled up at Matt, restraining an urge to give his hand a squeeze.

They stopped at the top of the hillock and looked down. The pond lay peaceful in the slight hollow, green meadow grass before it, a tangled mass of fern and trees beyond.

Slowly, they moved through the grass dotted with cowpies. White sweet clover and yellow buttercups smiled up at them. Purple foxgloves fringed the edges of the hollow, an occasional clump scattered among the other meadow flowers.

Matt let go of Sara's hand and scooped a foxglove into his palm. "See these tiny holes below the stem? Hummingbirds do that when they suck nectar."

Sara looked at the tiny holes in awe. "Really? I thought they were poisonous."

"It is, in large quantities. But in smaller doses, it's used as a heart medicine. Apparently, the birds don't get enough to harm them." He gestured toward the water. "Look."

The murky water rippled faintly with the movement of tiny creatures—dipping flies, darting water skippers, a jumping fish. Even as they watched, a male mallard left his wild snowball and willow cover to swim toward the center of the pond.

Mandy hopped with excitement, waving her pointing finger. A large brown turtle sunned himself on a partially submerged log. Before they could come closer, he slipped into the water and disappeared.

Mandy could contain her silence no longer. "It was real," she cried, "it really was!"

She sat down and pulled off her shoes and socks, then swiftly rolled up her blue jeans. Sara and Matt grinned at each other as they watched her wade into the squishy mud dotted with tall pond grass.

Matt nodded toward a dilapidated dock jutting out into the water. "Shall we?"

They walked together onto the sagging boards. Matt picked up a long stick and prodded a dark area in the water. A golden salamander surfaced, grabbing an apparent tidbit before vanishing again into the dark muck.

"I still think they're ugly," she said.

She looked across at the other shore. Wild pink roses and snowballs, their blossoms past their prime, hung over the water. Sara identified alders, willows, and some vine maples vibrant with bright pink seed pods resembling tiny airplanes.

She left the dock behind and turned toward the meadow, Matt beside her. A tiny blue flower winked up at her like a forgotten star.

"Wild forget-me-not," Matt answered before she could ask.

Sara watched a blue dragonfly sail low, noted a pair of swallows dipping in dance above the foxgloves.

Matt took his camera from its case and focused on a blackberry vine festooned with white blossoms and golden honeybees. He walked farther away and Sara was left alone absorbing the trill of an unseen bird and the whisper of the wind in the firs.

Suddenly she had an idea. *I'll find some flowers to sketch.* She picked a tall foxglove marked with a hummingbird kiss.

Smiling at her fanciful thought, she carefully snipped off a blue forget-me-not.

Mandy left the mud and climbed up beside her. "Oh," she exclaimed, "a tiny strawberry!" Then it was gone, popped between Mandy's rosy lips.

"I'm going to take these home and draw them," Sara said as Matt came toward her.

"Great." Matt ran his hand over his camera. "I captured a couple of pictures that I think will be special. One was a maidenhair fern dripping over the water; the other, believe it or not, is that wild blackberry vine. It has a certain aura about it."

Sara smiled. She felt she could have stayed forever in this quiet haven away from the stress of her life.

But Matt had to work that afternoon. He dropped his hand onto Mandy's head and started toward the pickup.

The drive back to town seemed too short. It was hard to face the old uncertainties after the idyllic morning.

When Matt stopped the truck in front of the house, Mandy jumped out and raced ahead in her usual impetuous manner, letting herself through the gate. Her dismayed cry brought Sara and Matt running.

She stood on the steps, an arm around Boris. He stood tall, yet somehow shamed, his neck bare of his great spiked collar. The front door gaped open.

"Not again!" Sara cried. "It can't be—"

They rushed through the door. The living room brooded silent and empty, the kitchen untouched. But upstairs in Sara's room, drawers were upturned on the floor and bed, her lamp was overturned, and Garfield lay stomach up in the middle of the bed.

"The camera," Sara cried. "It's gone!"

10 / Pursuit

Once again the Faulkner house teemed with action.

"I won't have it!" Mr. Faulkner exclaimed as he came in the front door. "One has a right to have protection from this kind of trouble."

Sara couldn't have agreed more. "But, Dad," she said, "it could have been worse. This time nothing was taken—except the camera I found, and Boris's collar."

Her father's fist slammed onto the edge of the table. "That collar is what makes me so mad. They were using Boris to flaunt their power, right in our faces."

The doorbell chimed softly, and Sara jumped.

"It's just Officer Peterson," Mother soothed. "I called him as soon as you told me about the camera and collar."

Dad opened the door. "Thanks for coming so quickly."

Officer Peterson nodded, his eyes searching the room. "Sara," he said, "are you okay?"

"Yes," she replied, grateful for the concern in his eyes. "But the camera is gone—the one I found at the accident scene. Dad, will you take him upstairs and show him where I had it?"

The two men disappeared up the stairs together. Matt and Sara went into the kitchen.

"I hate thinking of someone in my room, going through my things," Sara said. She opened the fridge and took out two Cokes.

Matt and Sara sat down at the table, sipping their Cokes in silence. Sara's thoughts kept returning to her room. Would something else turn up missing? What *was* happening, anyway?

She turned as her father and the policeman stopped inside the door.

Officer Peterson was encouraging. "I think this will be the last time, Sara. Somehow, I think you're onto something with that camera. I'm not sure what—"

Matt agreed. "Now that they have it, it's unlikely they'll be back."

But Sara shook her head. "They still don't have *their* film," she said. "They'll discover soon enough that the film inside the camera isn't the roll they want."

There was silence as each person digested the information.

Officer Peterson frowned. "I'll assign an extra patrol car. In the meantime—" He looked hard at Mandy. "Keep an eye on the little one."

After he left, the rest of the family gathered around the table. Mr. Faulkner turned to his wife. "You'll have to stay home tomorrow. We can't have these girls here alone."

Mother nodded regretfully. "I agree," she said softly. "I'll call Lucille and explain."

"What about Aunt Nina?" Mandy asked. "Didn't you say she wanted to come and spend a month with us sometime?"

Mother's eyebrows arched. "Why, Mandy, I think you might have something there. I wonder . . ."

Aunt Nina was delighted that her niece needed her. Alone, her two children grown and her husband gone, it was exactly right for her.

The Faulkner house exploded with a different kind of activity. Even though Aunt Nina was partially crippled and used a cane, she was never still.

She roasted chickens and baked bread. She washed windows, cleaned closets, and set the girls doing innumerable errands.

"Nobody would dare come near our house with Aunt Nina in it," Mandy grumbled, her arms loaded with jars for the basement shelves. "They wouldn't dare."

Sara looked out the sparkling clean window. Boris lay on the porch, his head on his paws, the picture of neglected love.

"Daddy should have gotten Aunt Nina instead of Boris in the first place," Mandy continued. "No one would dare take a spiked collar off *her* neck!"

"Mandy!" Sara reproved. Her lips twitched with suppressed humor. She could imagine her Aunt Nina meeting Boyd at the door, brandishing a broom. He'd back up for sure, probably falling over Boris in the process.

"Go get your jars put away, Mandy," she said.

Mandy stomped down the stairs. Sara could still hear her grumbles as she went out to join Boris on the porch. He looked up at her hopefully, his great tail thumping the wide boards.

"I'm sorry, Boris," she said. "Maybe when this is all over we'll get back to normal. Then you can sleep in my room."

She rubbed his ears thoughtfully as she remembered the afternoon she had stood and looked at her ransacked room. It *had been* horrible. But Sara had to admit, it had been freeing, too.

The mental vision of Boyd upturning her lingerie drawer and touching her personal items had made anger swirl inside her. Never again would a look from Boyd's dark eyes release butterflies in her stomach. Never again would his, "Come," find her stumbling in his footsteps, reduced to a helpless blob of compromise. She was free.

Except for Aunt Nina.

It was hard to find a quiet moment with Aunt Nina's restless spirit dominating the house. Sara had begun rising early for her tryst in the side yard.

Her robin was still there, plump, bright-eyed, intact except for the one leg that dangled helplessly. She stood in the grass, peering, thrusting with her beak, feeding, then fluttering forward. Sara marveled at her quiet courage and perseverance.

"She's a good illustration of the patience James talked

about," Sara told Boris who was stretched at her feet.

Boris lifted his head, nodded and lay back down, quietly watching the fluttering bird. He never bothered it. Once Sara saw him lunge at a neighboring cat lurking too close. She wondered if the huge dog and the small bird had some unspoken agreement between them.

Sara smiled. "You're a good dog, Boris. A little large, but a good dog just the same."

The telephone shrilled and Sara hurried into the living room.

"It's for you," Aunt Nina said, holding the receiver out to her. "Matt."

Sara took it. "What's up, Matt?"

"My bandage is off and my motorcycle's fixed," Matt said joyfully. "Want to go for a ride with me?" His voice lowered, "We could go house hunting."

Sara laughed. A picture of the turreted house in the photograph leaped into her mind. "I'll have to ask."

Aunt Nina stood in the doorway, a dishtowel flung over her shoulder, her legs braced. For a moment the mental vision of Boris's spiked collar encircling her neck made Sara's lips quiver. It would have been so fitting.

"Matt wants me to go for a motorcycle ride with him, Aunt Nina. If I get permission from Mom or Dad, could you watch Mandy?"

Aunt Nina snorted disdainfully. "Who's watching out for whom?" she grumbled.

"Why, you are, Aunt Nina," Sara said meekly. "We couldn't have gotten through this week without you."

Aunt Nina's taut shoulders relaxed. "Don't bother to call your parents, honey. Just tell him yes." She stomped into the kitchen mumbling, "Motorcycles, hot rods—in my day it was Saturday afternoons at the movies."

Sara giggled. Having Aunt Nina in the house wasn't all bad. Not really.

Sara was waiting on the porch when Matt roared to a stop. She ran out to him, eagerness flashing from her gray eyes.

Matt grinned back, noting with obvious approval her blue jeans, navy jacket, and plaid flannel shirt. "I'm glad you dressed warmly," he said.

He handed her a helmet and showed her how to fit it over her head and fasten the clasps beneath her chin. Then they were off, the wind pushing hard against Sara's visor, her jacket, and jeans. It took a while for her to relax—especially with her arms around Matt's waist. But after a few miles she felt comfortable. It was fun!

Matt slowed for a corner and turned to her. "Like it?"

"Yes! Except for the noise!"

"You'll get used to it!"

They left Sara's neighborhood behind and began to explore an area with tall, old-fashioned houses. Matt slowed. Intently, they studied each house, searching for tall turrets and narrow rectangular windows.

Matt pointed to a tree bending over a tall, white-columned porch. "That tree looks like the one in the picture," he shouted, "But the porch is all wrong!"

A car careened around them and momentarily distracted Sara.

"He's in a big hurry, Matt," she noted. "Watch him!" Her arms suddenly clutched Matt tightly. "Matt, that license plate. It's the one that I wrote down at the restaurant—"

"Are you sure?" Matt twisted the throttle and the motorcycle jerked forward.

"The car is different," she gasped, "but the number is the same. I know it is!"

Her words were lost as Matt accelerated. The car was just ahead of them now, a bright yellow and black Plymouth. Sara peered through her visor. All she could see of the driver was his dark, well-shaped head. He turned to one side and Sara felt sure it was Boyd. Or was it?

Her thoughts raced. What was the license plate from Hot and Sweet's Chevrolet doing on this car? She caught her breath as the motorcycle bore close to the Plymouth's rear bumper. The driver seemed unaware of their interest, intent only on hurrying through town.

He turned a corner and Matt followed. A red light loomed overhead, catching their cycle, but allowing the black and yellow car to go free.

Matt leaned toward her. "I'm still going to follow. I want to see where he goes."

The light changed, and the motorcycle jerked ahead. For a while Sara was afraid the speeding Plymouth had eluded them. Then she spotted it a few blocks ahead.

The chase continued through the tree-lined streets and onto the freeway out of town. Matt opened the throttle wide. The noise roared in Sara's ears. Her head began to throb. She leaned forward, pressing her face against Matt's shoulder.

She was unaware of which exit they took off the freeway, but when she lifted her head they were on a winding country road. The black and yellow Plymouth flashed ahead, like a goldfinch darting into the wind.

Sara knew then that the dark-headed driver was aware of them and trying to elude them. Her stomach sank as they whirled around each curve. The Plymouth suddenly roared onto a lonely gravel road to the left.

Matt braked and tried to follow. But the loose gravel caught the wheel. They spun to a stop inches from the side of a tall bank.

"We lost him!" Matt exclaimed. He jumped off the cycle and turned to help Sara. She got off stiffly. An unexpected trembling traveled through her body. She hoped Matt wouldn't notice.

But he did. Gently, he guided her fumbling fingers at the clasp on her helmet. He removed it and led her to the side of the road.

"I'm sorry, Sara," he apologized. "That was a rough ride. I shouldn't have."

Sara licked her dry lips and swallowed hard. "It's all right, Matt. I wanted you to chase him as much as you wanted to. Where are we, anyway?"

Matt waved his hands vaguely. "Up in the hills. I'm not

sure where myself. But don't worry. I'll get you home.''

A chill made Sara shiver. ''I almost hate to get back on,'' she confided.

Matt nodded. ''We'll wait, then go slowly. I'm sorry, Sara.'' He reached out and touched her hand. ''You're still cold.''

He took her hand in both of his and began to rub gently. ''Feel better?''

''I'm all right,'' Sara insisted, ''really I am.''

She gave him a wobbly smile that tried to reassure him but somehow failed. Matt's arm crept around her shoulder. Sara buried her face in his jacket and burst into tears.

They sat there a long time. After a while Sara looked up. ''I'm all right now, Matt.'' Her throat threatened to stiffen into a sob. She forced a smile. ''We'd better go.''

They walked together to the motorcycle and put on their helmets. But before Matt pulled her visor forward, he bent down and kissed her forehead.

''That's a promise,'' he said, ''that I'll get you home safe and sound. No more wild rides.''

Then he patted her cheek. ''And that's a promise that we'll both come back. I have a feeling it would be good for us to look around these hills. We just might find that yellow and black Plymouth.''

Sara felt like adding, ''And Boyd?'' but she didn't.

11 / Discovery

Sara lay in bed, too tired to sleep. Visions of motorcycles and speeding yellow and black cars flashed through her mind. So did endless curves, and driving wind, and— a warm arm drawing her close.

She sighed and turned restlessly onto her side, pulling her knees to her chest. The ride back into town had been long but carefree. They'd stopped at a wayside cafe and enjoyed a Coke, then explored a stream at a quiet rest stop. Before they got home, clouds had built up in the sky.

Sara could hear the wind's curious fingers probing her windowpanes. With the first gentle rain spats, the frogs in the pond began to rejoice. "It's here—it's here—"

Another answered, "Not now—not now—not now—"

"Foolish frogs," Sara reproved. She stretched her legs out long and again felt their weighty weariness. The croak changed, "He's here—right now . . ." The wind and rain and frogs soothed her. Sleep came quietly, gently, wrapping its dark cloak around her tired spirit.

Toward morning Sara dreamed. A tall house with turrets that cut into the sky rose before her. She walked toward it, even as sudden thunder growled and lightning bounced off its peaked roof. She stopped.

Aunt Nina's voice drifted up the stairs, accompanied by the steady banging of two metal objects. "You girls going to sleep your lives away? It's after nine and time to be moving! Look alive!"

Sara sat up, reluctantly pushing back her blanket. *After nine, and I promised Matt—*

She looked out the window. Thick clouds, tinted lavender from the thin, drawn curtain, covered the sky, blotting out the mountain. She shivered. *Summer rain.*

There was a light tap on her door. The door opened and Mandy pranced in, somewhat like a pony, her head thrown back, her feet dancing as though she walked on rubber.

"Mandy!" Sara cried. "Where did you get that blouse? Take it off at once!"

Mandy bounced to a stop and frowned.

Revulsion rose inside Sara as she looked at her. Mandy's innocent loveliness hid behind rouged cheeks and bright red lipstick, her large blue eyes outlined with matching shadow. The rose-patterned blouse Sara had tossed into the back of the closet mocked her. Somehow, Mandy had managed to tuck and smooth it until it clung to her girlish figure.

Sara glanced at her sister's neck. *Mandy knows better,* she thought. *She's taken off the cross.*

"You've been in my room," she stormed, "and you look—terrible—"

Mandy ran to her like a sudden summer rain. Repentant tears slid down her cheeks, making rivulets in her painted face. "I'm sorry, Sara," she cried. "I woke up early this morning and couldn't go back to sleep. I didn't have anything to do, so I came in here. And the next thing I knew—"

Sara hugged her little sister hard. "It's all right, Mandy. It's just that—I hate to see anyone dressed like that since—since—"

"I'll take it off," Mandy promised. She hugged Sara, then ran out the door.

Sara dressed slowly, reluctant to face the dreary morning. Would her robin be in the side yard? Would Boris be waiting?

She shivered and sat down on the edge of the bed instead. As she reached for her Bible, she thought of Matt steadily working his way through the book of Hebrews. She had tried to join him there, but it had been too hard for her. She could picture the glory of Christ in the first chapter but after that the warnings and exhortations blurred together, confusing her.

Reluctantly, she had returned to the book of John.

Now she opened to the fifteenth chapter. She could understand how Jesus was the Vine and she a branch. Her being in Jesus, and Him in her, was something she grasped more clearly now.

After a while she put her Bible aside and closed her eyes, trying to concentrate on her Lord seated on His throne. Instead, she saw the house in her dream rearing into the clouds. Mandy, dressed in a rose-patterned blouse, stood before it.

Sara's eyes popped open. "That's it!" she exclaimed. "We'll go house hunting. Mandy will love it!"

Mandy did.

Even Aunt Nina approved. "It'll do the young'un good to go traipsing about with her big sister. Why, when I was a girl—"

Sara and Mandy caught each other's eye and winked.

After nearly an hour of poring over maps and outlining potential neighborhoods, the girls set out. "You look nice in that blue-checked shirt and vest," Sara approved.

Mandy smiled. "Lots nicer than red roses, isn't it?"

Sara flushed and arched her eyebrows playfully. "What about me? Do I look better in turquoise blue than roses?" She lifted her chin and turned a half circle.

Mandy cocked her head and regarded her soberly. "Yes, you do," she said. "That color makes your gray eyes almost blue. And I like the way your pants fit—not too tight—and not too—"

Sara reached over and gave her a playful pat on top of her blond hair. "You're an observant little girl," she said. "I think you're just the person I need to spot that old house."

Mandy took Sara's words seriously. She sat on the bus with the picture on her lap, memorizing each detail.

"That big tree in the yard sort of leans toward the house, doesn't it?" she observed. Then a little later, "There are curtains on the main floor but not in the upstairs."

When the bus entered the neighborhood Sara and Matt had explored earlier, Mandy sat with her nose pushed against the window.

As the bus emptied, she stirred, "I don't see anything

that looks like it at all. Why don't we ask the driver?''

Sara nodded and made her way to the front of the swaying bus. The driver looked at the picture with interest as she held it out to him.

"No—not around here. But wait—" He scratched his head thoughtfully. "Have you ever looked in the Glisan District out in northeast Portland?"

Sara shook her head. A few minutes later, with transfers in hand, they caught another bus.

"This is fun!" Mandy exclaimed. "You can see so much more than when you're going through in a car."

Sara agreed. But she was getting tired. Portland was so large and there were so many out-of-the-way streets where a tall, ancient house could hide.

"It has to be a place where there are big trees," Mandy noted.

Sara looked thoughtfully at the maple-lined street. Something stirred inside her.

"Let's get out and explore."

Mandy stood up and Sara followed. She caught Mandy's hand as they jumped from the rear door onto the sidewalk.

"Let's go up that street," Mandy said eagerly.

The tall maples beckoned, rustling their leaves in invitation. Sara looked high above their branches, saw blue sky beginning to break through the clouds.

They started down the next block. The houses looked as though they had once been loved and cared for. But now an air of neglect prevailed. Sara noted a broken screen door, an unweeded flower bed, an old car parked in a driveway. All contributed to a general feeling of sadness.

Sara found herself wondering about the people living in the houses. Were they descendants of once well-to-do pioneer families? Or new families who could not afford to keep the neighborhood as beautiful as it once had been?

"The tree!"

Mandy's excited cry interrupted Sara's reverie.

They raced ahead, turning down another side street. There it was—a bit back from the street behind a tall, leaning maple, its rounded upstairs windows turned toward them, curtainless—

Excitement surged through Sara as she stared at the house. But her excitement mingled with a faint apprehension.

Mandy started to bound up the front walk.

"Wait!" Sara cried, plunging after her. She grabbed Mandy's hand, slowing her footsteps.

Would Boyd come to the door? Sara wondered. Or the blond boy she'd seen at the accident scene? And what about Hot and Sweet? Would he show up here?

The girls stepped onto the front porch. "Maybe we should wait until Matt can come with us," Sara said nervously. She pushed a strand of brown hair off her forehead, then lifted her chin determinedly. It was broad daylight. There was nothing to be afraid of. Besides, she didn't need to hide behind a man's protection.

Sara bravely reached out and touched the doorbell. She could hear it ringing in the depths of the house.

No one answered. She tried again. Still no response.

"No one's home," Mandy whispered. "Let's look in the window."

"We shouldn't," Sara reproved. Then curiosity overwhelmed her.

They tiptoed over to the window and peered through the white, lacy curtains. A couch and chair. An open book before the fireplace—

Sara gasped. "That vase," she whispered, "the one on the mantle. It looks like Mother's—the one that was stolen."

"Let's go inside and take it!" Mandy exclaimed. "They have no right—"

"Hush," Sara said. A car slowed on the street. She grabbed Mandy's hand. "Let's get out of here."

A sudden urge for action propelled them off the porch. For a moment Sara hesitated. Should they dodge behind the great overgrown shrub or walk nonchalantly down the walk?

She chose the latter. With their pace held to a decorous saunter, Sara hoped they looked like neighbors out for a friendly afternoon call.

No one seemed to notice. The car disappeared, the houses brooded in silence.

"Let's ask the next-door neighbor who lives there," Mandy suggested. "Maybe he knows something about these people."

Sara shivered nervously. "Oh, Mandy, I don't know—"

"Look!" Mandy cried. She pointed across the street. An elderly man leaned over the top of his shovel, arms folded, quietly watching them.

Sara's fingers tightened on Mandy's. "Don't point, Mandy. It's rude." She had a sudden impulse to give her little sister a quick kick, but stifled it. "Let's just go over and say hello."

Mandy's hands jerked to match her bouncing footsteps. "Maybe he can tell us—"

Sara shot her a warning glance. "You let me do the talking," she warned. "Hush!"

Sara pasted on a neighborly smile as they crossed the street. The man watched them, his gaze steady, though not unfriendly.

"Good afternoon," Sara called.

The gray head nodded, a faint smile creasing his face. "Afternoon's gone," he said regretfully.

The girls stopped. Sara gestured toward the house they'd just left. "No one's home."

"Ah, no," the old man mused. "Edna's gone visiting her sister in Tacoma. She won't be home until tomorrow or the day after. You relatives of hers?"

Sudden pink dyed Sara's cheeks. Mandy's fingernails dug into her sister's palm. "Not exactly—"

The old man frowned. "You stay away from Edna Schaffer's nephew, young lady. You hear? He ain't good news."

He thrust his shovel aside and turned away, his thin shoulders taut with indignation. Mandy and Sara looked at each other as the old man disappeared around the corner of the house.

"Boyd," Sara murmured, "now I know where you live."

The girls walked back to the bus stop—but not before Sara turned to the towering house for one last look, one last promise.

"We'll be back when Edna Schaffer is home, old house. Matt and I will come together."

12 / The Salt Marsh

Matt's reaction to Sara's discovery of the old house was depressing. Or was it Aunt Nina's disapproving countenance as she stood in the kitchen doorway, brandishing her cane in one hand and a rolling pin in the other that made Sara's spirits plummet?

"In my day, boys called girls," she said loudly.

Sara's cheeks burned. She clutched the receiver tighter, hoping Matt hadn't heard Aunt Nina's strident voice.

"It was clever of Mandy to find the house," Matt said softly. "But I've been thinking. What does it prove? They might just have liked the way it looked."

Sara wet her lips. "I—we—Mandy thought she saw mother's cut-glass antique vase—"

"Are you sure?" Aunt Nina snorted. "There's lots of cut-glass vases around." Her cane thumped across the linoleum as she retreated back into the kitchen.

Sara breathed a deep sigh of relief.

"I think you should call Officer Peterson," Matt said. "Of course they would need proof before they could go snooping around."

"Do you think maybe you and I could?" she asked. "I mean go back—snoop around ourselves."

A sudden silence hung between them. Sara could almost reach out and touch it. "Matt?"

"I'm here, Sara. Just thinking." His sigh winged over the line and settled into Sara's heart, a heavy, weighty thing.

"Tomorrow is my day off," he said.

Sara's heart thudded with hope, which was soon dashed by his next words.

"What I'd like to do is to get away. The wildlife at the

salt marsh is special, and I haven't been there in ages. To-morrow may be my only chance with that crazy schedule I have at work.''

Disappointment stirred inside Sara. "That's all right, Matt," she said bravely. "I—I suspect the old house will keep.''

"It isn't the house I'm worried about, Sara. I need to go back to where we lost that yellow and black Plymouth. Something inside me tells me that's more important.''

"Then why don't you? Go back, I mean—''

Matt laughed. "Because the sandpipers are piping, and ducks are calling, and seagulls are flying, and I''—he lowered his voice theatrically—"must go,'' he said. "Want to go with me, Sara?''

Sara's pulse quickened. A day with Matt would be a day apart—away from Aunt Nina's disapproval and Mandy's demands. But the house . . .

Sara longed to return to its towering stateliness. She was sure it contained her mother's missing camera and film, their stereo, the heirloom vase. She wanted to go back, but not alone. She needed someone with her who knew her God.

Something ugly twisted her stomach into a knot. Would they also find the tall, dark-haired boy whose attraction had begun all the trouble in the first place?

"How about it, Sara?'' Matt was asking. "Do you think your parents would approve of a day's trip to the salt marsh? It's close to Nehalem Bay. We could get there in a few hours.''

"I—I think they'd approve. Dad's beginning to act as though he trusts me—especially when I'm with you.''

"Then how about it? We could take Mandy.''

But I'd rather not, Sara wailed inwardly. *I'd rather it was just the two of us, alone. And I'd rather go to the old house.*

Aloud she said, "Oh—okay—I'll ask.''

Matt didn't seem to notice her hesitation. "Great!'' he exclaimed, "I'll call you tonight.''

Sara, Matt, and Mandy stood together on a green, grassy knoll, the morning blueness tipping around them. *It's like the inverted bowl you read about in books*, Sara thought, *its edges fringed in green—thimbleberry bushes, elderberries, tangled blackberry vines. After that the marsh grasses stretched to the sea and sky.*

"I camped overnight here once," Matt confided. "The next day I went down to the marsh, and took some branches and covered a frame that the hunters use during duck season. I stayed inside most of one morning—duck watching."

"Did you really see them, without them knowing you were there?" Mandy asked.

"Did I ever!" Matt made winging motions with his hands, and the three of them scurried down the path.

As they neared the bottom, salmonberry vines caught at their jeaned legs. A bird flew low over their heads, as intent as they to reach the open marshes.

Sara watched Matt ahead of her on the path. Sunshine streamed through the leaves and rested in a patch on his light brown hair. She caught her breath. It was almost as if God were touching him.

A long blackberry vine clawed at her shoulder, drawing her concentration away from him. She withdrew the thorny tendrils carefully, observing the trees bordering the path. They were bound together with blackberry vines and nettles—an impenetrable, inhospitable place. Sara shivered and continued down the path.

Mandy galloped in the lead, her long, blond hair streaming below her shoulders. Sara pushed her own shoulder-length mop from her neck and blew at several stray hairs wandering by her nose.

She quickened her pace. Matt turned and looked back. "You okay?" he asked, his smile radiant.

She nodded breathlessly. *He's glad to be in his beloved woods,* she thought, *even though it's full of stinging nettles and clutching thorns. It's where he belongs.*

They kept going until the nettle-bound woods were behind. The marshes, edged with driftwood and debris, lay before them. Matt bent over a rotting log patterned with blackberry leaves and white flowers.

"Sara," he called.

Overgrown salal waved, bending young green tendrils toward Sara, brushing her arm. "What is it, Matt?"

Matt knelt beside the stump as she joined him. Sara noticed another log ahead of him boasting tangled garlands of honeysuckle waving orange trumpets.

"Hmm, lovely," she murmured.

But Matt wasn't looking at the flowers. His slim brown fingers untangled a fine gold chain from a branch. "It's a cross," he said with wonder. "Someone's lost a necklace."

Nostalgia moved inside Sara. She knelt beside him. "It's like the one I gave to Mandy." Their eyes met. "I shouldn't have."

She leaned back, bracing her hands on the soft earth bordering the path. Briefly, she explained why she'd given her cross to Mandy the night of his accident. "It just didn't go with what I was doing—sneaking out with someone I hardly knew—letting my parents down."

Matt nodded. "Isn't it funny how an object that represents Jesus can be used to remind us of Him when we need Him most?"

"Except I didn't want to be reminded right then. But you're right. It did bring conviction in the end. I miss it dreadfully."

A faraway look gathered in Matt's eyes. "I carved a cross once and gave it to my brother. I was only ten. I always wondered if it meant anything to him. Especially later—"

"Did he—"

"I don't know." The blue-gray eyes that reminded Sara so much of an ocean mist, deepened into dark pools. "My brother went away from God, Sara. He lives in Portland. He's into marijuana—booze—"

Matt's fingers touched the gold cross in his palm. "That's where I was going the night of the accident. He keeps moving from place to place, never telling us where he is—only occasionally getting in touch. That night he'd called."

"What does your brother look like? I mean—"

"Tall, skinny. When I was little I used to call him hawk-face. Made him so mad—" He turned.

Mandy, jumping from log to log, came toward them. "What are you two doing?" She spotted the cross lying in Matt's palm. "Oh," she said, one hand going to her neck. "It's beautiful—more beautiful than mine."

"It's for your sister," Matt said. He smiled at Sara, then leaned forward and clasped it around her neck.

Sara swallowed with difficulty. "Thank you, Matt."

The day now stretched before her with promise. It didn't matter that a faint rotting smell from the tide flats mingled with the fresh salt-sea smell, nor that Mandy pulled at her hand, beseeching her to hurry. This day was all she imagined it would be and more.

Sara knew the endless grass, the calling ducks, and the friendly clasp of hands would be tied together in her memory with a strand of gold—her cross.

Twilight found the three of them—tired, dirty and content—climbing back to where they'd parked the pickup.

"Whew!" Sara exclaimed as she and Matt leaned back against old Doc. Mandy wandered a short distance away and sat down, her face lifted heavenward.

A silence fell over them as they watched the intense blue of the sky being transformed into the pinkish purple color of flushed plums. Sara stared a long time before she realized there were stars hidden in its depths.

"First star I see tonight, I wish I may, I wish I might," she quoted, then paraphrased, "have the prayer I pray tonight."

"Sara," Matt's voice was as soft as the twilight. "I didn't want to say anything sooner, but something happened at our house last night—something we need to pray about."

Sara turned her attention from the gleaming golden star. "Yes?"

"Last night someone tried to break into my darkroom—"

Sara gasped. "But that's impossible. How could they connect—us?"

"I wondered that myself. Then I thought of that yellow and black Plymouth we were following. He *could* have gotten my license number—somehow found out who owned the motorcycle. It's registered in my name."

"And you've been to my house. If they were snooping around— Matt, was anything taken?"

"Nothing. But they sure scared my mom to death. She was all alone when she heard this scrabbling noise. She thought it was the cat, and it made her mad. Nothing makes her more angry than a cat trying to get inside the house. And we have one like that." He laughed. "Sneaky—heads straight for the kitchen. Anyway, Mom got up to investigate, saw a light outside the window, and let out a yelp. Whoever it was, left."

"How awful," Sara said. She remembered her own fears in the night and shivered. Then another emotion rose inside her. "Does this mean that we'll check out that old house together—soon?"

Matt nodded soberly. "Yes, it does, Sara." He shifted his arm until it rested behind her shoulder. "I should have gone back to where we lost that Plymouth this morning. Then we could go to that house tomorrow. But," he gestured wordlessly at the dying day.

"Mrs. Schaffer may not be home until later," Sara reasoned. "We'll get more information if we wait until we can talk to her."

"Maybe . . . but, Sara, I need to apologize. I was being insensitive to those break-ins at your house. I knew they were terrible, but I didn't realize how vulnerable they make a person feel. To have strangers actually inside your home, going through your things . . . Your family is handling it well. I admire you."

A sudden lump swelled inside Sara's throat. "Not so very well," she whispered.

Matt's hand reached out and covered hers. "Sara, let's pray. Right now."

Sara nodded. "The Lord's been telling me that He's near to those with broken and crushed hearts. And now"—she searched for the right words—"I think I'm learning a little bit of what He meant."

She looked up at Matt in the pink dusk. His hand tightened over hers.

"Sara," he whispered, "there's something special about broken places, at least those our Lord heals. Afterward, the broken spots are stronger than ever."

Hope as tender and golden as the newborn stars overhead flooded Sara's being. She bowed her head.

"Lord, thank you for being near to me," she said, "for fixing the broken places in my life. And thank you for Matt's caring, and my parents' trust in me again, and these golden stars—"

Matt's deeper voice continued her prayer. "Lord, we need your help. We're caught up in something we don't understand. Will you guide us, please? Show us what to do. Protect us . . ."

Memories of plum-colored skies wrapped around Sara as she snuggled beneath her covers that night. A deep peace curled itself around her spirit, born from more than the end of a perfect day—born from the prayer she and Matt had prayed together in the purple twilight.

That winking gold star had been far distant. *But God dwells within me, spreading comfort into all the nooks and crannies of my life,* she thought.

Sara turned onto her side, pulling sleep around her like a blanket. Her last thought before tipping into dreams was, *He's here, right now.*

The song her frogs had sung before the rain was her song now.

13 / In a Dark Wood

Sara opened her eyes to a morning devoid of purple twilight and golden winking stars. Instead of frogs croaking gentle messages, Aunt Nina's demanding tones hustled her into wakefulness before she was ready.

Aunt Nina is an irritant, she decided. *There isn't any way you can get around it.* Nevertheless, she pushed back the covers.

"The housework is always with us," she groaned to herself in the mirror. "Why all the rush?"

She dressed quickly. The sun-drenched morning inspired blue jeans, a candy-stripe blouse, and gold clips to accent her brown hair. She touched the gold cross at her throat and smiled at the girl in the mirror.

"Now all I need is a green frog on something. He and my cross would remind me that my God is near—always. Maybe I could paint one on a T-shirt."

Household chores claimed her morning: breakfast, dishes, vacuuming. It was midafternoon before Sara, Mandy, and a guilty-faced Boris skipped into the side yard.

"You're lucky," Mandy complained. "You get to go off with Matt while I"—her head bobbed toward the house—"I have to be here at *her* beck and call. I've a good mind to take a book and hide in the ivy tunnel."

A protest leaped to Sara's lips. "You wouldn't—"

Mandy shrugged and walked over to the grape vines rambling over the fence. "Actually I could make a tunnel in here." She parted the leaves and peered inside. "Aunt Nina would never know."

Sara sighed and sat down on the wooden bench. Boris

stretched at her feet, cradling his great heavy head across her tennis shoes.

"It's after nine, Boris—way after. But I don't think God minds. I wish Aunt Nina—"

She opened her Bible to John 15. Somehow, it seemed fitting that she linger in the vine chapter.

"Abide in Me, and I in you. As the branch cannot bear fruit of itself, unless it abides in the vine, so neither can you, unless you abide in Me.

"I am the vine, you are the branches; he who abides in Me, and I in him, he bears much fruit; for apart from Me you can do nothing."

"That's you talking, Lord," she said.

She looked up. The dark-green ivy gleamed in the sunshine. Mandy played contentedly, hidden beneath the grape leaves on the back fence. Sara could hear the soft murmur of her voice.

She read again. "If you abide in Me, and My words abide in you, ask whatever you wish, and it shall be done for you. By this is My Father glorified, that you bear much fruit, and so prove to be My disciples."

Sara's gaze returned to the grape vine. "I'd like that much fruit, Lord. I wonder if there are tiny, hard green grapes forming there now."

She sighed. "It takes time for them to grow, doesn't it? I wonder if it will with me—"

She closed her Bible and pulled out a spiral notebook. A grape leaf formed beneath her pencil, then an ivy leaf.

"I'd rather be a grape vine than ivy, Boris," she said absently. "The much fruit kind."

Her fingers hesitated and then began a new picture; a huge frog with big round eyes stared back at her.

The slam of Matt's pickup door brought her to her feet. She grabbed her jacket and the two rattled off.

Leaving the freeway, they began exploring unfamiliar, winding country roads. They hesitated at each curve, noting each crossroad.

Matt braked to a stop. "It was right here that he ditched us."

Sara nodded wordlessly, remembering the steep bank and Matt wiping up her stupid tears.

Matt's eyes darted eagerly from one side of the road to the other. "I don't think he realized at first that we were following him," he said.

"But, Matt," Sara protested, "I still don't understand what we're doing here, not really. What *are* we looking for?"

"I don't know." He flashed her a grin. "But the way that guy was driving, he knew these roads like I know my camera. Sara, that road to the left—let's follow."

He jerked the wheel and turned sharply. Vine maple and hazel branches scraped the sides of the pickup. Matt leaned over Sara and rolled up the window to keep the intruding branches from slapping her. "They sneak up on you," he explained.

He slowed the truck, easing it over the deep ruts and holes which tossed them from side to side.

"Don't worry about this road, Sara," Matt reassured. "Dad and I are explorers. I was raised on back roads like these."

An extra-deep rut thrust Sara's head to the roof, then jounced her firmly into the padded seat.

"Ouch!" she giggled. "You might have been raised on roads like these, but I—I'm lowered on them!"

After that it was hard to realize the seriousness of their mission. The pickup rocked with a delightful combination of laughter, ruts, and corny jokes.

They sobered as the road ended in an open field fringed with alders, willows, and towering firs. Cars in various stages of abandonment cluttered the meadow. They leered grotesquely at Matt and Sara, some devoid of headlights and bumpers, others without tires or fenders.

"Is this a junkyard?" Sara asked unbelievingly.

Matt shook his head and turned off the ignition. "I don't know," he said slowly, "but I'm going to find out." He opened his door and stepped out. Sara followed.

At the far end of the field towered a tall oak tree. A motor swung on a pulley from one stately limb. Matt and Sara walked toward it.

"Wow!" Matt exclaimed. "This is some place."

"Kind of spooky—"

"Not really. I wonder what this place is used for. Look, Sara. That old truck, it has a pulley on it, too."

Sara looked past his pointing finger. A strange contraption on the truck bed thrust its T-shaped nose into the air, the pulley dangling from one arm like a broken wing.

"I'm going to take a closer look," Matt said.

Sara held back uncertainly. "I'd rather we didn't. Somehow—"

Matt stopped. "Come on," he urged. "Nobody will care."

Sara shook her head. "It isn't that. Do—do you think this place has anything to do with—that yellow and black Plymouth—and Boyd?"

Matt shrugged. "Hard to say. But it fascinates me."

"Someone has been here recently," Sara observed, noting the worn areas around the truck, the fresh tire tracks. "How long do you think these cars have been here?"

Matt didn't answer. He moved toward the truck, eagerness in the set of his shoulders and buoyancy of his walk. Sara watched him for a moment, then turned toward the car nearest her.

She peered through the windshield, trying to find the registration. But the car was only a gray shell. The seats were gone, the floor boards stripped, the steering wheel bare.

Sara backed away, lifting her eyes to the surrounding woods. An incline rose sharply to her left. "I bet I could see the whole yard from up there," she whispered. She could imagine herself telling Matt the number of cars and their exact locations.

She turned toward the hillock and began to climb. At the top, she looked down. Cars of every description filled the clearing, spilling into the forest.

It's an eerie place, she thought. *Dead car bodies—skeletons—*

She moved down the other side of the hill, quickening her pace. The trees closed in around her. *Strange, here no one would ever dream that a car boneyard was close by.*

Afternoon sun slanted through the trees, making leaf patterns on the moss and brown fir needles. She could hear the rustling of leaves, the whir of tiny wings as a bird flashed past. She wandered farther into the forest.

The verses she'd read that morning about much fruit returned to her. She tipped her head back to look for fir cones. A tingle went through her as she discovered some small, hard, green cones not much bigger than her thumb.

The trees aren't even struggling to grow them, she marveled. *They're just here, living, growing, producing what they were created to produce—without struggle—in quietness and simplicity.*

She was so deep in thought that she failed to notice the sun dip behind the treetops. Wonder stirred in her as a soft, brown-feathered screech owl swooped low. It lit on a fir branch ahead of her and cocked its head.

Sara smiled. She advanced toward it softly, holding her breath. As she came within several yards of it, the owl flew away, lit on another branch, and peered down at her.

Again Sara moved forward. Again it flew. This time it disappeared, lost in the darkening woods.

Sara stopped, consternation filling her. Dusk was falling. She was far from Matt.

She turned to retrace her footsteps. After a while she stopped again. Was she going in the right direction? She looked up, but the trees stood like identical, silent sentinals wrapped in dusky aloofness.

Sara scowled. She noted vine maples clinging low to the ground, ferns brushing her jeans. They hadn't been there before, or had she not noticed?

"Am I really lost?" she whispered.

The soft wind sighing through the firs was her only answer.

Determinedly she went on. "I'm sure I came this way—or did I? Lord, I need help—your help—" Her anxious eyes probed the woods. "There were alders and willows there, I think—"

Hope surged through her as she spotted the tiny leaves of a willow peeking out from behind a fir. Realization that the field was just beyond sent adrenalin rushing through her. She ran toward the clearing, then stopped.

Half-hidden by alder saplings and willow branches was a dark green Chevrolet with front windshield and fenders missing. She started to shout, "Matt!" then shut her lips. She moved forward slowly, softening her footsteps.

She had to look inside the car, see if she could discover if it had once belonged to Hot and Sweet.

A branch caught at her hair. A fallen limb tangled her feet. Still she crept forward. She stopped at the driver's side and looked in the window.

"It can't be—" she whispered. "It can't be—"

She took a deep breath. Boris's spiked collar lay on the seat just out of her reach.

Cautiously, Sara looked around. The hulking shapes of nearby cars seemed to draw closer, menacing her. Fluttering shadows danced in the dusk.

Sara's hand reached out and woodenly clasped the door handle. It swung open. As she slid beneath the wheel she thought she heard the willow branches behind her move.

A twig snapped.

14 / Attacked

Sara's fingers closed over the spiked collar. Cold dread squeezed her heart. The burglar? Boyd? Hot and Sweet? Any one of them could be near.

She squinted nervously through the darkening woods. No menacing shadow lurked close, no sound but the gentle whisper of faintly moving willow leaves.

She opened her lips to call Matt, then closed them, reluctant to shatter the hovering quiet. Clutching the collar with one hand, she reached for the door handle with the other.

It swung open and she jumped to the ground, her legs feeling like jelly. Her foot slipped.

A long arm from nowhere wrapped around her, pinning her arms to her body. Her tennis shoes skidded on the soft leaves of a downed willow branch. She almost lost her balance. Something tightened about her arms, jerking her back against a tree, and she dropped the collar.

Sara heard a mutter behind her. She twisted her body, trying without success to see her captor. Her lips opened in a cry only to be silenced as a twisted bandana gagged her mouth.

Her unseen assailant jerked the handkerchief into another knot, then quickly tied her hands to the tree. Picking up the spiked collar, he retreated, fallen branches crackling beneath his feet. Sara strained her ears and bent as far forward as the rope allowed.

Her heart thudded. Would he return? "Oh, Matt!" she cried silently. "Where are you? Are you all right?"

Sinister silence, then a motor throbbed. Gradually the

sound faded into the distance. The dark woods closed around her.

Sara trembled. If only she could break away and find Matt. She twisted her hands, her body, then sagged against the tree.

"Sara! Sara!" Was there panic in his cry?

A great mumbling groan fought its way past the bandana. *Oh, Matt, Matt—I'm here*—her thoughts gasped.

He came toward her in the dusk. Then he was beside her, his fingers fumbling with the knot at the back of her head. The bandana dropped from her mouth.

"Matt!" she cried. Her hands strained against the rope.

"Don't," an unfamiliar voice said. "You'll make it tighter."

Sara tensed as his fingers grappled with the knot.

"I can't get it," he grunted. "Wait—" A slight pause, then, "I'm going to cut it with my knife. Hold still."

The cold knife blade pressed against her wrist. The rope slid from her hands.

She whirled around to face her rescuer. The long, hawk-like face she'd memorized the day she found the camera looked down at her. She started to open her mouth, but he silenced her with a shake of his head.

"Please," he said, "don't tell Matt."

He turned and strode into the woods, his broad shoulders taut and squared. Sara stared after him, confusion tumbling inside her.

"Sara! Sara!"

This time she knew the tall figure coming toward her was Matt's own. She turned and ran to him. Then she was in his arms crying unintelligibly of spiked collars, unseen burglars, and unidentified attackers.

Matt held her gently, patting her shoulders. "Don't worry," he reassured her. "Everything's going to be all right."

It took a while for Sara to regain her composure. "I know," she whispered. "It was just so scary. So—" She had a sudden desire to divulge the near presence of her rescuer, but his "Please, don't tell Matt" restrained her.

Matt's arm tightened around her shoulder. "I know," he said. "But Sara, the pieces are beginning to fit together."

Sara rubbed the tears off her cheek with her palm and looked at him. "What do you mean?" she asked.

"After you wandered into the forest, I took a good look around. Sara, this is an illegal car-stripping operation. And—are you ready for this? I think the photos in the camera are evidence that these"—he waved his hand around the clearing—"are being made into new vehicles."

Sara nodded her head. "It makes sense, Matt." She suddenly remembered the spiked collar. "Boris's collar!" she exclaimed. "I found it." She related how she discovered it inside the Chevrolet parked beneath the willow.

She shuddered. "I think Hot and Sweet attacked me. Or Boyd. The evidence of the collar would link one of them to the break-in at our house, the camera, and eventually the accident."

Matt agreed. "This is probably why whoever hit my motorcycle took off so fast. They knew that if they stayed, the police would discover the car wasn't right. It looks like they forge registrations and everything. Of course their plan is bound to have holes in it." He shuddered. "This whole thing looks pretty bad—dangerous, too." He looked behind him. "Let's get out of here."

"Yes, let's." She reached up a hand to squeeze the one lying protectively on her shoulder. "Thanks, Matt—"

His hand closed over hers. "Come on, Sara."

With clasped hands they returned to Matt's pickup. On the way down the winding road, Matt turned to her.

"Sara, where did you go? After I'd looked that truck over, I started to get frightened. You were nowhere around."

Sara smiled sheepishly. "First, I looked inside a car shell, then I decided to find out what I could see from the top of the hill. There was a screech owl," she confessed. "It kept flying from tree to tree—actually fluttering would be a better word—"

Matt grinned his understanding. He turned off the steep

gravel road and onto smooth pavement. "Shall we go to my house first? Take a look at those photos?"

Sara nodded. "Yes, let's. But, Matt, we still can't prove *who* tied me to that tree."

"No," Matt agreed. "Nor did you see who crashed into my motorcycle. But *they* don't know that."

Sudden fear closed around Sara's heart. "They've seen me, watched me. It makes me feel strange—"

Silence filled the cab. Somehow neither of them were willing to put the rest of their thoughts into words.

The night closed in around them. A golden star winked shyly from the top of a fir before disappearing into its branches.

Sara's old star prayer breezed into her thoughts. *Star light, star bright, first star I see tonight, I pray I may, I pray I might, have the prayer I pray tonight—that we might be able to put a stop to these strange happenings—without anyone getting hurt. Please, Lord.*

The warm light spilling from the windows in Matt's house comforted her.

His mother welcomed them with a "Goodness!" as she led the way into the kitchen. "You two look worn out."

Sara nodded wearily as Matt took up the tale of the car-stripping operation in the woods. His mother gasped when he told how Sara had been tied to a tree.

"But that's awful!" she cried. "Terrible. We must report it right away!"

Matt shook his head. "First, we want to have a look at those photos again. Both Sara and I think they're important—maybe evidence against those involved in the illegal car stripping."

The three of them hurried into Matt's darkroom. Matt turned on the light and stepped to the table. His long, slender fingers leafed quickly through a pile of photographs beside the developing tank.

He frowned. "Mom," he said, "the photos aren't here. I was sure—Did you move them? Put them somewhere?"

"I haven't been in here, Matt," his mother replied gently. "Could you have left them in your room?"

The frown deepened on Matt's forehead. "I was sure I left them here," he grumbled.

"Why don't you look in your room, Matt?" Sara suggested. "It's easy to misplace things."

"Especially if you're as absent-minded as my son," his mother teased. Matt was still scowling as he left the room.

"I'm that way, too," Sara defended, "especially when I'm working on lots of things at once."

Matt's mother shook her head. "It doesn't seem to matter how few or how many. Matt walks around with his thoughts skyward. Sometimes I wonder—" She laughed suddenly. "I'm sorry, Sara. Matt *is* an unusual boy. And I appreciate him."

She smiled as her son rejoined them, but there was no answering smile from him. Worry darkened his face.

"Mother, have you been here all day? Have you seen anybody around?"

His mother paled. "What is it, Matt? What are you thinking?"

"The photos. They aren't in my room—anywhere." He looked at Sara. "Are you thinking what I am?"

Sara took a deep breath. "Probably," she said hesitantly.

"What are you two talking about?" Mrs. Roberts demanded.

"We think someone has broken in here and taken the photos." Matt spread his hands wide. "I'm sure they were right here—on this table— just last night."

A thoughtful look deepened in Mrs. Robert's earnest, gray eyes. "I left for a while," she said. "But not for more than half an hour."

"I'm going outside," Matt said. "I want to see if there's evidence of anyone coming through a window."

His mother shook her head. "I didn't lock the door when I left. If anyone came, they could have walked right in." She tilted her head. "Funny, I didn't notice it then, but Freda—she's my pet parakeet, Sara—Freda was chattering and horribly upset when I got back. I wonder—''

''If only birds could talk,'' Matt mused.

''But they can't,'' Sara said practically. ''I think we should call Officer Peterson. He'll know what to do.''

''Right. Besides, he has a copy of those prints, too. Remember?''

Sara nodded.

Mrs. Roberts led her to a small birdcage in her bedroom while Matt went to the telephone. Freda hopped back and forth on her perch, her green and gold feathers fluffed into an agitated ball.

''She's still upset,'' Mrs. Roberts said.

''Pretty bird—pretty bird,'' Freda squawked, her beady eyes sparkling.

''Why, she talks!'' Sara exclaimed.

Mrs. Roberts laughed. ''But of course!''

''Pretty bird—pretty bird. Dave's gone—Dave's gone.''

''And who is Dave, you nonsensical bird?'' Sara rested her hand against the wire cage. Freda pecked at her fingers. ''Ouch!'' Sara cried. ''You naughty bird!''

''Freda, be kind to our guest,'' Mrs. Roberts rebuked the parakeet. ''Sara, you come into the kitchen when you're finished visiting,'' she said, turning to the door.

Sara nodded. ''Talk, Freda,'' she commanded. ''Tell me who Dave is.''

But this time Freda merely looked indignant. She hopped into the far corner, ruffled her feathers and refused to even look at Sara.

''Silly bird,'' Sara murmured. But no amount of persuasion could induce Freda to turn around.

Sara joined Matt and his mom in the kitchen just as he related his phone conversation with Officer Peterson. ''He thinks we're onto something big!'' Matt exclaimed. ''Of course he didn't say that, but I could tell.''

Opening the refrigerator, he took out a carton of milk, poured two glasses, and motioned for her to join them at the table. ''Officer Peterson wants to talk to you, Sara,'' he said. ''You're to call him as soon as you get home.''

Sara shivered. Somehow she felt she'd rather leave the dark woods behind her. The memory of those grasping arms, the handkerchief tightening around her mouth—

She reached for the glass of milk, then set it down abruptly. "I'd rather not," she blurted. Her eyes met Matt's. She took a quick breath inward. There was something in his glance—a tenderness, a gentleness—

She looked down at the tablecloth in sudden confusion, not knowing what to say.

Matt reached across the table and touched her hand. "Instead of my taking you home, would you rather we made a quick trip across town to see a certain old house?"

Sara looked up quickly. His flashing smile reassured her, pushed back the dark forest with its tentacled shadows. Her own hand turned over and clasped his.

"Please," she said. "I'd like that."

15 / "My Boyd"

The monotony of the freeway and the drone of traffic lured Sara into daydreams. Memories of the fluttering owl, the towering T-shaped nose of the tow vehicle, its pulley dangling like a broken arm, made her shiver.

"Are you all right, Sara?" Matt asked. "Maybe I should take you home."

Sara pulled her thoughts away from the dark woods. "No," she said. "The old house will help me forget. Besides, I can't help but feel it'll bring us one step closer to proof." Her voice lowered. "A proof that will tie everything together. I hope I can find it in the dark."

"We'll find it," Matt assured her. "I looked at a map. Sara—"

She looked at him expectantly in the darkness, but he lapsed into a troubled silence. Sara could feel the unrest nibbling at his spirit. *It's beginning to affect me, too*, she thought. *Can it be that he's afraid of something I don't understand? That he doesn't really want to find out who's behind this crazy three-ring circus?*

She pushed her thoughts aside and concentrated instead on freeway exit numbers. They easily found the old house. It brooded alone behind the streetlights, its tall, narrow windows dark in the night.

"I don't think anyone's home," Sara said nervously.

Matt peered through the windshield. "I think I see a light in back."

He got out slowly. "Coming, Sara?"

She pushed hard on the handle and joined him on the sidewalk. "I hope Mrs. Schaffer isn't in bed."

"It's not that late," Matt assured her.

"But for an older lady—"

Matt took her arm gently. "Would you rather go home?" he asked.

Sara shook her head. "No," she said. "I want very much to meet Boyd's Aunt Edna. And I'd like a closer look at that vase, too."

Slowly, they walked down the narrow sidewalk. Sara remembered an edging of cheery yellow marigolds, but in the darkness it looked more like the outlines of a slithering snake.

"The light is coming from the kitchen," Sara observed in a low voice. "I remember—"

They stepped onto the porch and knocked. Soon the soft pad of footsteps was followed by the fluttering of a curtain. "Boyd?" a voice questioned.

"N–no," Sara stammered. "I'm Sara, Boyd's friend—"

The door opened. An elderly woman with thin gray hair curling around her face peered at them. Sara noticed her big, capable hands, the thrust of her long jaw.

"I'm looking for Boyd."

The woman's steady, colorless eyes examined Sara quietly. "You're too pretty a girl to come looking for my Boyd No, not too pretty. Too sweet."

Matt stepped close behind Sara. "Sara knew him from the drive-in where she worked," he explained. "She hadn't seen him for a long time, and she was worried."

"Over my Boyd?" Disbelief echoed in the old woman's voice.

Sara studied her closely, noting a look of patient endurance that enveloped her like a cloak.

"We—I knew him rather well," she explained. "And then—all of a sudden he was gone. I was wondering if he was all right . . ." Her voice died into an uncertain silence. She didn't know what else to say.

The old woman seemed to understand. She stepped aside, motioning them to enter. "You'll have to excuse my surprise," she explained. "It's just that no one ever comes here asking about my Boyd. He's my nephew, you see. And he's always had such a time making friends—except for Dave and Roy. They come sometimes—and Boyd's other uncle—"

Her keen eyes examined Matt with open curiosity. "You aren't much like the others who have been here—except for Dave."

"Dave?" Matt asked. He leaned forward, a look of concern clouding his usually fine features. "Dave who?"

Boyd's aunt only shook her head sadly. "I don't remember last names very well. But it's funny, you two do have a look about you. Same coloring, except his hair's lighter, but the general resemblance is there. Now about my Boyd. You say you were worried?"

Sara licked her lips nervously. "He'd often come to the place I used to work. Then he asked me to meet him and—and—"

"He didn't show up."

"Right. Something happened that night, and I thought—"

"There was a hit-and-run accident," Matt explained. "Sara was concerned that Boyd might have been involved—since she never saw him again."

The old woman nodded. "I see," she said, "I see. But, I hope he's not in trouble Miss—Miss—"

"My name is Sara Faulkner. And this is Matt."

"Sara. It's a good name. You can call me Aunt Edna, both of you. And about my Boyd, he's all I have left," her voice dwindled. "I sure hope he hasn't done anything wrong."

Unbearable pity for the old woman grew within Sara's heart. "I'm sure he loves you," she stammered.

There was an answering gleam in Aunt Edna's eyes. "Oh, yes!" she exclaimed. "I know he does. And sometimes he shows it, too. Not in big ways, but little ways. Like the vase—"

An unexplainable feeling burned in Sara's throat and squeezed it like a vise. She shot Matt an agonized glance, but he didn't see. All his attention focused on Aunt Edna.

"A vase?" he asked. "Did he give it to you as a gift?"

"Let me show it to you," Aunt Edna said. "It's really

very old, I think. The cut glass has a purple haze that indicates an antique."

She stepped back from the alcove and disappeared into the gloomy living room.

"Matt," Sara whispered, "you shouldn't have—"

His look of utter incredulity stopped her. "I thought you wanted a closer look."

"I did then, but now— That poor old woman—"

She stopped abruptly as Aunt Edna came through the door, proudly clutching a cut-glass vase in her hand. "My mother had one of these years ago. But it was broken. Boyd must have remembered."

Sara took the vase with trembling fingers. "It's beautiful," she breathed. "I'm so glad you showed it to us." She extended it to Matt, a pleading look in her gray eyes.

His fingers touched the glass lightly. "I bet it's beautiful when the sun shines through it," he said gently.

"It is," Aunt Edna assured him. "Several days ago I filled it with roses from my garden. They were white with a slight pink tint, and somehow the violet hue—" She took a deep breath, clearing her throat self-consciously. "To think my Boyd—"

"I—I—" Sara stammered, "I think we'd better go now, Aunt Edna. We—" She returned the vase to the old woman, patting her big, weather-beaten hand impulsively.

The old woman grasped Sara's hand and squeezed it warmly. "You're a nice girl, Sara. I appreciate your caring enough about my Boyd to come." A sudden shadowed look veiled her colorless eyes. "But, honey," she whispered, drawing her away from Matt's questioning eyes, "you stay away from my Boyd. He's special to me because he's all I have. But dearie," she said, nodding toward the door, "he don't hold a candle to that boy back there."

A sudden warmth colored Sara's cheeks. "Could I come back?" she asked. "Not—not to see Boyd—but to see you?"

The old woman's chin raised with dignity. The colorless eyes shone with character and refinement.

She's known better days, Sara thought with unexpected

understanding. *But life has been hard for her. I wonder if I could be her friend.*

Aunt Edna nodded as though reading her thoughts. "You could come for breakfast some morning," she said. "I always eat about nine. And I get lonely."

They joined Matt in the alcove. Aunt Edna still clutched her cherished vase. Matt opened the door. The woman stood still, smiling at them, her eyes peering at Sara. "You come again, Sara. You don't have to call. Just remember, breakfast is always at nine."

They left her standing there.

"Oh, Matt!" Sara cried, when they were alone in the car. "It was so sad. And that vase. It is Mother's. But I'll never be able to tell her."

"You're sure?"

Sara nodded. She leaned back stiffly and closed her eyes. "I think *I* have troubles; then I see someone whose life has obviously been one long disappointment after another."

She opened her eyes. "I wish I could think of something awful to do to Boyd. But that would only hurt her more."

"Sara," Matt rebuked, "Boyd's already in for a heap of trouble. First, the hit-and-run, then, breaking into our houses, and now that car-stealing operation."

"We can't prove it!" Sara cried.

"We will," Matt said grimly. "We will, whether we like it or not."

16 / Aunt Nina Wields Her Cane

Matt's vows to prove Boyd's involvement "whether we like it or not" tormented Sara.

No matter whom it hurts? Oh, that poor old woman—Aunt Edna.

Sara's thoughts boiled relentlessly. She edged her shoulders next to the door of the pickup and stared into the night. There were car lights coming—always coming, streetlights and neon lights glaring harshly.

Back in the clearing there would be moonlight mingled with starlight, a gentle, caring light, except it would glisten on an ugly dangling pulley, glint off broken cars.

"Don't, Sara," Matt entreated, reaching across the open space between them.

Sara drew farther into her corner. "Please, Matt. I need to think this through—" her voice caught, "alone."

Matt withdrew his hand. He looked straight ahead, paying extra attention to his driving.

Now I've done it, Sara thought. *I've turned him away and I didn't mean to.* She closed her eyes and leaned back in the seat. *Oh, Lord, help me sort out my tangled feelings. Help me see what you are trying to teach me.*

Gradually, her emotions quieted. In her mind she drew a picture: a tree, a branch, an apple. Across the apple she printed just one word—trust. She knew that trust involved giving Aunt Edna into God's hand, trusting Him to bring healing into her life.

She looked up, startled, as the pickup stopped in front of her house. She turned to Matt. "I'm sorry. After everything you've done—for me to go on a 'we can't hurt the poor, old woman' trip—"

Matt lowered his head, his hands stroking the steering wheel in troubled silence. "Sometimes we have to make decisions that are right but painful," he said at last, "instead of wrong and comfortable."

Sara watched his hands move restlessly around and around the steering wheel. "Matt, what's bothering you? Really bothering you? It isn't just Boyd and those awful stripped cars, is it?"

Matt grasped the wheel tensely. He took a deep breath, and his chin sank to his chest. "No, Sara. It's—my brother, Dave—" His voice lowered. "I never told you. I hate to tell you now."

Sara slid across the seat in one quick motion. Her hand reached out and touched his cheek.

Matt caught it, holding it tightly. "I think—my mother and I think—that he's the one who came into the house— took those pictures."

"But—" Sara protested.

"I know it sounds preposterous," Matt said. "But it's not as much as you'd think. Sara, I told you he lives in Portland, but what I didn't tell you is that he rents an upstairs room near where you live. That's where I was going the night I was hit. At first I didn't connect him to it, but now I do. He knows who hit me, Sara. I'm convinced—"

"He's the blond I described, the one who watched our house that morning?"

"Yes. But I didn't realize—not at first."

"Is that why you sort of—you know—seemed almost reluctant to—"

Matt nodded. "Remember when we followed the yellow and black Plymouth? I recognized Boyd that day as Dave's friend and began to wonder. I didn't want to think that my own brother knew who had struck me down and wasn't saying anything."

He sighed. "I feel much the same way you do about Boyd's Aunt Edna." His hand knotted into a fist. "Oh, why do the innocent have to suffer with the guilty? Why is it that when a person sins, he always hurts another?"

A lump formed in Sara's throat. She remembered her strange benefactor in the woods and started to speak. She shut her mouth quickly. He'd said, "Please, don't tell Matt." She hadn't understood then, but she did now. He was Dave, Matt's brother. He didn't want Matt to know he'd been there.

"I think," Matt pursued, "that Dave is involved with Boyd and this Hot and Sweet character. But of course I don't really *know*."

I do, Sara wanted to cry out. *But what if I'm mistaken? Couldn't it be a mere coincidence that he was there?* Her thoughts circled like a baying hound treeing its prey.

He's kind, she thought. *Couldn't he have been there trying to protect us both from his friends?* "It's getting late," she said. "I'd better go in. Dad and Mom went out, and Aunt Nina's alone with Mandy."

"I'll walk you to the door," Matt offered. He got out and opened the door for her, holding out his hand.

She took it quietly. Somehow, their relationship had deepened. Their few moments of sharing had drawn them closer. They didn't need words as they walked up the steps and across the porch.

Sara reached for the doorknob, but her hand froze in consternation. A scuffling sound came through the closed door. She raised frightened eyes to Matt, then pushed the door open. A sharp exclamation and a dull thud propelled her through the living room and into the kitchen. She reached for the light switch.

The sudden light dazzled her eyes. "Aunt Nina!" she cried.

Aunt Nina perched triumphantly on a kitchen chair, her cane hooked around the neck of a man sprawled on the floor.

"I hit him good!" she cried, "and now I've caught him!" She gasped as the man began to thrash violently. "You're going to have to help me!" she screamed.

Matt pushed past Sara and bent over the intruder. The man turned his head.

Sara recognized the beefy face, the flashing eyes. "I

know you!'' she cried. ''You were there the night of the accident!''

The fat man's lips drew murderously thin. His lips twisted and he spat straight at her. Sara turned her head quickly.

Matt slammed his fist into the big man's jaw.

''Call the police!'' Matt hissed.

Sara grabbed the cane. ''Please, Aunt Nina,'' she gasped.

But Aunt Nina cried, ''I've got him!'' and landed on all fours in the middle of his paunchy stomach.

After that, it was easy for Matt to twist a dishtowel around the groaning man's hands while Sara stood ready with the cane. Aunt Nina escaped to the next room and began to dial. Hearing her excited words, Sara caught Matt's eye and smiled ruefully.

''He's here in the kitchen, right now,'' Aunt Nina explained over the phone. ''I caught him myself. Why, I heard him come into the dining room while I was in the kitchen.

''I'd just come down for a drink and I couldn't find the light switch. Anyway, it was dark—real dark. I heard this noise in the next room, so I climbed up on a chair and waited. When he came within reach, I hit him with my cane. I put his neck right there in the crook of my cane and kept fighting him—''

''I wish I could see their faces,'' Sara giggled. ''Do you suppose they've ever had a more unusual report?''

Matt smiled, but there was a poignant hurt behind it that made Sara wince. She went over to the sink and turned on the water, splashing its fresh, cleansing warmth over her cheeks. Even though the fat man had missed, she wanted to be sure that not even a trace lingered.

Officer Peterson and another policeman arrived quickly. Sara and Aunt Nina let them in, and Boris pushed his way in behind them.

In her excitement, Aunt Nina talked nonstop as Sara led the way into the kitchen.

Aunt Nina's captive was sitting up, his eyes smoldering. ''I'm not the only one in on this mess,'' he said belligerently. ''I'll give you names—for a price.'' His sweeping gaze rested on Aunt Nina. "And that old hag," he said. "I can sue her!"

Sara's eyes flew to Matt's face. She saw her own consternation mirrored there.

"Names won't be necessary," Officer Peterson said quietly, "not with price tags. And neither are threats."

Sara stepped back. "I'll be in the living room if you want to question me." She took Aunt Nina's arm. "We both will."

She turned and left the men alone, thankful to be away from the fat man's dark gaze, grateful for Boris's presence beside her. The couch's softness welcomed her.

Boris came close, resting his beautiful brown muzzle in her lap. His dark eyes adored her.

"Where were you when we needed you?" Sara chided. She laid her hand between his ears. "You have your own set of problems don't you, Boris? Just like I have mine—"

She looked up at her aunt prowling restlessly from window, to piano, to the door. "Come join me, Aunt Nina," she invited.

But Aunt Nina couldn't stop her pacing. She thumped her cane against the carpet and turned anxious eyes kitchenward.

"I hope they get my side of the story," she grumbled, "not just his."

"They already have, Aunt Nina," Sara reassured.

Aunt Nina turned her hand over and studied it. "I didn't know I had that much strength. I didn't even think about it. I just did it."

She frowned. "It hurts now," she said as she flexed her fingers experimentally. "I hope his neck hurts worse."

"Did he say anything?" Sara asked. "Before you hit him, I mean—"

Aunt Nina snorted disdainfully. "He didn't have a chance. From the moment I hit him with my cane, all he could think of was leaving the neighborhood. I hope he's learned his lesson."

But Sara's thoughts had taken wings. She knew she would

have to tell Officer Peterson about her experience in the dark woods. She'd have to tell him about Matt's brother.

Her dread increased as she wondered about the ugly spitting man with Matt and the policeman. Why had that curious fat man of the accident scene come into their kitchen? What had he been trying to do?

Sara shivered and sank deeper into the couch's softness.

17 / Withered Branches

A dirty bandana swayed from a dark branch. A dog barked. The handkerchief changed into a broken spiked collar dangling from a swinging ivy vine.

An unexplained hope leaped in Sara. She reached for the vine only to have it elude her, swinging farther and farther away, yet ever closer. Just as her hand closed around the collar, it disappeared. The ivy wrapped its long tendrils around her, and she was falling—falling—falling—

Sara jerked awake. Her blanket twisted uncomfortably around her body, and she was hot and sweaty.

She struggled loose from the confining blanket and straightened her legs. Somehow, the ceiling seemed too low, the night too dark. She got up and pushed her curtains aside. A faint breeze from the window touched her cheeks.

The dark, heavy feeling persisted. *It must have been the dream*, Sara decided. *That, or last evening's excitement*.

Matt had been so quiet. He'd left with only a faint nod in her direction.

Then Officer Peterson took her aside and she told him everything—the stranger in the dark woods, Aunt Edna's Boyd, and how she and Matt had been fitting the pieces together.

Officer Peterson said little. He merely nodded and wrote. He had left with his customary assurance, "We're watching out for you."

Sara sighed. The ivy below her glinted silver in the moonlight. In her dream it had come closer—closer—

She switched on the light and reached for her sketchbook. If she could capture the vine on paper, it wouldn't be so threatening.

The vine grew beneath her fingers, not an ugly, menacing creation, but a fairy-like work of art, weaving itself around the edges of her page. After a while she turned off the light. She could sleep now.

She wakened with a thought. "I suffered on the cross that you might know Me intimately." She lay very still and let the warmth of it creep around her heart. One hand stole out and picked up her Bible.

She turned onto her side, drawing up her knees. "Jesus said He was the Vine," she mused, "and I a branch. That means He wants to be close to me—my own special friend."

Her vine chapter reached out to her. Once again the "much fruit" phrase filled her with yearning.

She stopped reading, and her thoughts whispered, *Just let Him live out through me, His strength, my strength. Lonnie, Doreen, the customers at the drive-in—someday I'll work there again, only it will be different. His love, my love, somehow so simple and yet so complicated.*

She read on, "This is my commandment, that you love one another, just as I have loved you. Greater love has no one than this, that one lay down his life for his friends.

"You are My friends, if you do what I command you."

Tears dampened her lashes as she underlined the verses carefully. Then she lay back, closing her eyes. *Love one another. Friends. Since Jesus is my friend, I can be a friend to others.*

When Sara slipped out of bed the next morning, she knew what she must do.

The scent of roses greeted Sara as she turned onto the path leading to Aunt Edna's door. Although it was almost nine o'clock, dew still lingered on the roses' red, gold, pink, and white upturned faces.

Sara lingered, delighting in their fragrance and colorful beauty, prolonging the moment until she would have to face her uncertainties. Aunt Edna spared her the agony of waiting.

The door opened, and Sara looked again into the rugged,

haunted face of the old woman. The sunshine unpityingly accentuated deeply-etched wrinkles in her weather-roughened face.

She held the door open wide, squinting in the morning light.

Sara held out her hand. "Good morning, Aunt Edna. I've shamelessly taken you up on your breakfast invitation."

A smile broke across Aunt Edna's features. "Sara," she said, "my friend in the night. Come in, come in."

Sara's fears evaporated at the old woman's obvious delight in seeing her. She smiled and followed her inside, looking around curiously.

The kitchen was a wealth of homey clutter, the counters and walls strewn with odds and ends of miscellany. Sara's roving eye picked out a cookie jar in the shape of a huge baby chicken, a snowy white teapot, a needlepoint wall hanging filled with a colorful assortment of cards and notes. Sara suspected they each held a memory.

Aunt Edna stepped to the stove and opened the oven. "It's my favorite kind of pancake," she explained. "It spreads itself in my skillet without any attention, while I go about as I please."

She drew the blackened fry pan from the oven while Sara sniffed in appreciation. "I've fruit to put inside, and presto—there's breakfast fit for a king." Her big hands slid it onto an old blue willow platter.

She opened the refrigerator and took out a bowl of fresh fruit. Sara leaned forward. Peaches and fresh blueberries mixed together with apple slices and frozen strawberries.

"It looks wonderful, Aunt Edna."

"It is. And so easy. Now all I do is pour my coffee." Her hands halted in midair. "But, tell me, child, what do you drink? I have—let's see—"

"Just a glass of ice water," Sara said quickly. "I can't think of anything that would go better."

"Or cost less," Aunt Edna said shrewdly. "I think we're going to like each other, child."

The hot, fruit-filled pancake disappeared rapidly as Sara

and the old woman hastened to get acquainted. They laughed, and chatted, and Sara soon forgot the intent of her visit. She even pushed aside the old woman's relationship to the man she and Matt suspected of several serious crimes.

"Aunt Edna—" Sara began. "I wonder—"

Suddenly the door opened, and Sara felt an instant sinking sensation. It flooded through her, plunging her downward—downward. But mingled with her fear came a whisper of thought. *I am your friend. I will never leave you or forsake you.*

Her chin thrust upward. "Hello, Boyd," she said quietly. "I'll bet you never expected to find me here."

Boyd stared at her. The enticing look that had once turned her to formless butter was gone. His brown eyes glowered at her from a face grown hostile.

Aunt Edna set her coffee cup down. "I'm sorry, Boyd. I'm afraid we've eaten everything up. If you had told me—"

"It's all right," Boyd said evenly. "I was just looking for a cup of coffee."

Sara leaped to her feet. She grabbed a cup from the mug tree and filled it with steaming brew from the pot.

He took the cup without a word and slammed out of the room.

"He has no manners," Aunt Edna sighed. "I've tried to teach him, but by the time I got him it was too late." She shook her head, "too late—"

"It's never too late," Sara said gently. "Aunt Edna, could you show me your roses? Tell me their names? I'll help you do the dishes later."

Aunt Edna leaped at the suggestion. "Let's," she agreed. "Dishes we always have, but mornings like this—" She picked up a pair of garden shears and guided Sara toward the backyard.

"I never dreamed—" Sara cried in awe. A flaming flower design dominated the green lawn. Its center was a circle of yellow roses, its petals of variegated colors: yellow, white, salmon, peach, and of course, red.

Like my blouse, she thought, *the one in my closet. But*

these roses are natural, beautiful, thrusting their blossoms toward their Creator.

As they walked among the flower beds, Aunt Edna told Sara their names and something of their history. "It's my hobby," she explained. Brandishing her garden shears, she clipped as she talked. Dead blossoms fell silently to the ground.

"I grew roses when my own children were growing up," she said, "and now Boyd encourages me to do the same."

A lump came up in Sara's throat. *He can't be all bad if he likes Aunt Edna's roses.* "Your children," she said, "tell me about them."

Aunt Edna smiled sadly. "They're both gone. My son was killed in Vietnam, my daughter in a car accident not long afterward." She reached out and patted Sara's shoulder. "Don't look so sad, child. It happened long ago."

"And your husband?"

"Gone—when the children were still in school." She gestured toward the porch. "I've been cutting back that overgrown wisteria vine," she said. "It made me feel bad. Like my family, those branches are cut away—gone—forever."

Sara turned. The vine clinging to the porch had obviously covered much of it before beginning its ascent into the tall maple tree. But now many of its branches hung limply.

They walked over to it. Aunt Edna reached up and pulled a withered branch forward. "See?" she said. "Cut off—dead."

She dropped the withered branch onto the ground and pulled a leafy one forward. "This is my Boyd," she explained, "the only one I have left." Her colorless eyes sharpened. "And now, Sara," she said softly, "I think you've been trying to tell me something, something I don't want to hear—about my Boyd—"

18 / Princess of Laughter

Sara stood alone in the rose garden. It was behind her now, their suspicions expressed. But her devastating words had been coupled with a quiet assurance. As she looked at the withered vine on Aunt Edna's porch she'd recalled John 15. Somehow, she wanted to communicate what she had learned.

"You don't have to be alone," she explained to the stricken woman. "When a person has Christ, that person has life." She pulled her sketchbook from her purse and opened to the ivy vine.

Aunt Edna's trembling finger touched the leaves gently as Sara explained the intimacy of the vine and the branches, of Jesus Christ and His followers. When Aunt Edna turned back toward the house, Sara ripped the page from its place and pressed it into her new friend's care-worn hand.

Now Sara covered her face with her hands. Matt's words hammered inside her. "Sometimes we have to choose what is right but painful, instead of wrong and comfortable—" And then the words of her Friend, "Sara, Sara, I am with you always—always—"

She shivered and looked up as a sudden shadow chilled her arms and shoulders. Boyd stood between her and the sunshine, his arms folded menacingly.

"What did you tell her?" he demanded. "Why?"

Sara raised her chin. "Why?" she repeated. "Because the police will be here soon, asking questions. I know it all—the car stripping, the hit-and-run accident."

She took a step toward him, holding out her hand in a pleading gesture. "Why don't you give yourself up, Boyd? You'd have a chance then. And Aunt Edna—"

Sara gasped as an unseen arm grabbed her brutally and thrust her hard against a maple tree. Someone's arm circled her waist while a hand clasped roughly over her mouth.

"You thought you could have it all your way—" Sara recognized Hot and Sweet's low voice. "Maybe you have another think coming."

Frantically, Sara twisted against his arm. But his strength was too much for her. She went limp.

A dim mist clouded her brain, distant voices intensifying her confusion. She struggled desperately, whispering, "My Friend—my Friend—"

Slowly, the terrifying mist cleared. She lay on a lawn chair surrounded by faces that strangely faded in and out. Everything seemed unreal.

"Matt," she whispered.

"I'm right here," Matt assured her, "and so is Officer Peterson."

Another face, looking oddly like Matt's own, swam into view. Only this face was long and thin. Confusion totally engulfed her, and she closed her eyes. Voices, there were too many voices, explaining, droning, going on and on.

The voices receded. When Sara opened her eyes again, she and Matt were alone. The leaves overhead whispered softly. They told her of faraway woods, of meadows and ponds, of birds and woodland tunnels.

In her imagination she could see a tunnel stretching through the woods. Honeysuckle and roses escaped from a garden arched above the treetops. Plumes of white, wild clematis foamed beside them. The light filtering down dappled the inside with green and gold. Shifting sun spots flickered like butterflies.

"I wish I could go there," she said dreamily to no one in particular.

A robin trilled. Was it her robin? The one who had tried to teach her perseverance?

Something moved close to her. The sunlight coins trembled.

"Sara," Matt's voice said, "are you all right?"

"Yes," she answered.

"Where is it you want to go?"

"Your tunnel, Matt. The green and gold one where the birds flicker in and out—and the chipmunks start up like little engines, chittering and chattering."

She closed her eyes again. "On second thought, I think I'd better get up."

Matt's hand touched her cheek lightly. "Take your time, Sara. There's no rush."

But there was. Boyd, Hot and Sweet, Matt's brother and Officer Peterson had all been there while she . . . She sat up. Instead of a tunnel she was under Aunt Edna's big maple tree, surrounded by roses. Beside her, withered, dead wisteria branches littered the yard. Matt knelt beside her, a worried frown squinting his eyes.

"Matt," she cried, "what happened?"

Matt reached for her hand. He held it while he detailed his and Officer Peterson's arrival and the subsequent arrest.

"We caught Hot and Sweet attacking you, Sara. Boyd just stood there. It was terrible."

Sara shuddered. "Poor Aunt Edna," she whispered.

"She's all right, Sara. In a way I think it was a relief to her. Sometimes knowing is better than guessing."

"Matt, your brother. I saw him here. I know I did."

"Yes, Dave was here. But in that case, I guessed wrong. And I couldn't be more thankful."

The hand clasping hers trembled slightly. "He wasn't involved with Boyd or Hot and Sweet, at least not in the way I thought. He was sleuthing them out on his own, even though they were his friends." His voice lowered, "—because of me, because of you."

"I know," Sara said. "Remember last night when we were in the clearing? Dave came to me and cut me loose."

"But I thought you'd—"

"No. Hot and Sweet—or was it Boyd?—tied me too tightly. I couldn't get away. I didn't tell you because Dave asked me not to. Besides, I didn't *really know* he was your brother—not then."

probable guardian of the camera. Boyd talked Hot and Sweet into searching your house each time—''

"The collar!" Sara exclaimed. "The stereo!"

"And your grandmother's vase," said a gentle voice behind her.

Sara turned, withdrawing her hand from Matt's. She started to take the vase that was extended to her, then shook her head.

"No, Aunt Edna. Not now. I want you to keep it for a while. I'll talk to my mother. She'll understand."

Aunt Edna smiled. "I don't really need it, child. But if it makes you feel better, and if it's all right with your parents, I'll hang onto it. It'll remind me of you and your promise to come again."

Sara rose to her feet and embraced her. "Oh, Aunt Edna. I'll come once a week. We'll talk and eat breakfast—''

The old woman nodded. "I'll look forward to it, then. You're a lovely girl. And I think a real friend."

She went back inside while Sara stared after her wistfully.

"I think you have something fine going with her, Sara. Don't fret. Our Lord will help us find answers."

Sara sighed heavily and sat back down. "I know He will. Now, where were we?"

"Let's go to the yellow and black Plymouth. I told you I recognized Boyd as Dave's friend. I began to wonder if Dave was somehow connected with the break-ins at your house and the initial accident. It really hurt me—my own brother."

"And he was?"

"Yes, but not like I'd imagined. Dave told us he was the one who took the photos from our house. His roommate was getting ugly, telling him he'd better produce or his little brother and his girl—would be hurt. Boyd and Hot and Sweet were getting nasty, too.

"That was the reason Dave had been skulking around the clearing. He knew Boyd's uncle, Boyd and Hot and Sweet, had a junkyard where they fooled around. But he didn't know the extent of the operation until last night.''

"And now we all know," Sara murmured. "Including the police. I'm glad—glad that it's being stopped."

"So am I. Something else, Sara. Before Boyd left, I told him we'd look out for his Aunt Edna. I couldn't tell for sure, but I think he was touched.

"Dave went to the police station with them, too. He told me he wanted to help if he could. Somehow that made me breathe easier. And Sara, I'm happy about something else, too.''

Sara looked at him quickly, then lowered her eyes. "What, Matt?''

"Us," he said simply.

"What made you—I mean, how come—?"

Matt smiled. "Are you asking me what drew me to you, Sara? At first it was simply your name.''

"My name? Sara? Matt, you'll have to do better than that!''

"I will! Let me explain. Several years ago I saw something in the life of Sarah in the Old Testament that changed my own life. Remember how quarrelsome she could be, and how mean she was to Hagar?''

Sara nodded. "Go on."

"I read something in Hebrews 11 that really threw me. Sarah—that mean, ruthless lady—was called a woman of faith! I went back to Genesis, determined to find out why.''

"And did you?''

Matt nodded. "I saw how she laughed at God in unbelief while sitting in the tent. And then I found something else—in a name.''

"Wow. You must have done some real research."

"I did. Isaac's name means laughter. Somehow after the time Sarah laughed in unbelief, God changed her, transformed that laughter into believing laughter.''

"That's right!" Sara exclaimed. "She laughed when God said she would have a son when she was too old.''

"But see how God transformed her attitude? At her son's birth, she said that his name would be Isaac. And that all

142

who saw him would laugh with her!''

"And her name is in the hall of faith in Hebrews 11,'' Sara marveled, ''because she finally recognized that without her God, she could do nothing—that she was totally dependent on Him for everything.'' Sara's fingers stole to her cross necklace. ''—even the changing of her attitude.''

"Yes,'' Matt agreed. "Sarah truly is a picture of God's grace, a princess of faith and laughter.''

"A princess? Where do you get that?''

"From her name. Sarah means princess.'' He smiled at Sara and she knew he wasn't thinking of the Sarah in the Bible. A flush rose in her cheeks as he drew her close to him.

She felt very special to be Matt's princess of laughter.